DEEP SPACE
DRAGNET

ALEX P. BERG

BATDOG PRESS
KNOXVILLE, TN

Batdog Press
www.batdogpress.com

Publisher's Note: This is a work of fiction. Names, characters, places, and incidents portrayed in this novel are a product of the author's imagination.

Cover Art: Damon Za
Book Layout: ©2013 BookDesignTemplates.com

Deep Space Dragnet / Alex P. Berg — 1st ed.
ISBN 978-1-942274-19-3

1

"A little more to the left," I said. "Just a hair. That's it. Perfect."

The mover bots' hydraulics hissed as they settled my clear plastic-wrapped couch into place. As the oversized sofa's legs met the floor, the mover bot closest to me retracted its forks and folded them into its body. It spun on heavy duty tires until it faced me. Gears whirred as it pulled its wheels up to mid-calf, simultaneously settling its feet onto the floorboards.

"Jay's Relocations is our name, but satisfaction is our game," it said in a tinny voice. "Is there anything else I can do for you today, Mr. Weed?"

The bot stood in front of me, roughly the same height as my own meter seventy-five and with a candy-apple red Jay's Relocations decal splashed across its torso. Between its retracted forklift tines, high load index tires, and solid frame, the machine better resembled a dune buggy than a droid. Nonetheless, it possessed the same minimal capacity for humanoid interaction any other dumbbot on the face of Cetie had, and, being a bot, it would do whatever I demanded of it—assuming I asked it to move furniture and paid the eponymous Jay in advance.

"Actually, now that you mention it," I said, "I think I'd rather have the desk ten to fifteen centimeters closer to the windows. I sat while you brought the couches up, and I found I wasn't getting as much natural light as I'd hoped."

"At your service, Mr. Weed," said the bot. "But could you provide a more precise measurement?"

Dumbbot, indeed. "Let's try twelve centimeters."

The mover bot sunk back down onto its wheels and drove toward my desk with its partner in tow. As they readied their forks, I heard Carl's familiar, measured voice behind me.

"You know, Rich, I have to admit—I had my doubts about this location, but upon further review, I concur with your choice."

I found him at the windows, which stretched from floor to ceiling across the entire southern face of my office in a single, unbroken sheet. His perfectly coifed short blond hair sparkled under Tau Ceti's bright mid-afternoon light. An aquamarine blazer gave shape to his shoulders, one that would have him soaked with sweat after a couple minutes in the Cetie heat—assuming he had sweat glands. To my knowledge, he'd never gotten the upgrade due to its expense and questionable functionality.

I joined him at his side. "It's the view, isn't it?"

"Well, that *is* part of it," he said, his gaze trained on the skyscrapers and space elevator of Pylon Alpha, the latter clearly visible in the distance from the forty-fourth floor of our new office. "But beyond that, I accessed some of the city's publically available seismology reports. As it turns out, this building is slightly farther from a fault line than our last office, and given its height, it's subject to stricter construction codes. In the unlikely event of an earthquake, my calculations show we'd have a two-point-six percent better chance of survival here than we previously would've. In addition, I scanned the flight patterns of incoming and outbound aircraft from the Cozy Harbor regional airport, and—"

"Carl...just go with it."

He turned to face me and smiled. His sharp blue eyes, optically superior to mine in every way, twinkled. "Sorry, Rich. It's the view."

He's almost as dense as you sometimes, said Paige in the back of my mind. *I'm not sure I'll ever understand his unique brand of synthetic consciousness.*

Because you're not truly conscious, I replied. *You're a few billion lines of code in a servenet buried deep beneath the bowels of Pylon Alpha.*

Paige delivered a mental sniff into my subconscious. *Wow, you sure know how to talk to a girl.*

I snorted, causing Carl to glance at me out of the corner of his eyes.

"What are you and Paige saying about me this time?"

Dang, he was good. I was sure Paige had kept him out of her most recent Brain communication based on his lack of response—she tended to only insult *me* to my face—but he'd figured it out anyway. I guess when you've known a guy for eighty-five years you tend to have a pretty good idea of what's going through his mind.

"What?" I said. "Nothing. Paige was telling me about how her own calculations give us only a two-point-five percent improved chance of survival in the event of a cataclysmic earthquake."

He's lying, said Paige.

"I can tell," said Carl.

As much as I loved my Brain—the cybernetic implant which let me take part in lifelike supersensory virtual experiences, connected me to the near-infinite collected knowledge of the known sentient races, and allowed me to play repetitive tile matching games when I got bored—I did sometimes tire of Paige's presence. She came as a sort of package deal with the Brain. After all, I couldn't run search queries or make Brain calls or operate the coffee machine all by myself. I needed Paige's digital consciousness imprint for those things. If only she weren't so *sassy* all the time...

Need I remind you, said Paige, *you brought this on yourself.*

"I know, I know," I said. "I chose your personality parameters once in the bygone days of yore. If I didn't want to be constantly razzed, I shouldn't have picked bubbly and cynical as your two primaries."

A tinny voice sounded behind me. "Mr. Weed? Does the placement of the desk meet your wishes?"

I glanced at it, now positioned so the afternoon Tau Ceti sun cut across it at a rakish angle. "Looks great. Thanks."

"Excellent," droned the mover bot. "Is there anything else I can do for you today, Mr. Weed?"

I looked around at the rest of my new office, which was about twice the size of my old one and an order of magnitude more expensive given the location. After my previous digs had been blown up at the hands of crazed Diraxi zealots, the multistellar corporations who'd been simultaneously investigating the incident insisted I take a sizeable payment to ensure my silence on the matter. I'd told them I wasn't interested in their money, but they hadn't listened. Of course, there were worse ways to spend a bonanza of SEUs than upgrading my professional storefront.

My splurge hadn't stopped at the signing of the lease. My new desk measured two and a half meters long and half again as wide. Its cherry wood construction meant it weighed a metric ton, and the fact that cherries didn't grow well in the Cetie heat meant the thing cost a fortune. I'd paired it with floor-to-ceiling cherry shelves that covered my entire east wall, and on the opposite side, I'd had the movers install a new item: an all purpose espresso and beverage bar, replete with an assortment of exotic liqueurs. A four piece couch and club chair set, which rested on a massive rug of lab-grown fox fur, completed the ostentatious look. Now all I needed was for the engravers to drop by and carve the words 'RICH WEED, PREMIUM INVESTIGATIVE SERVICES' into the door.

I gave the mover bots a nod. "Just unwrap the cellophane from the sofas and you can be on your way."

The bot droned on about how satisfaction was his game as he and his pal got to work.

I turned back to Carl. "You know, I think this calls for a toast."

He shot me a raised eyebrow. As much as I imagined myself the master of those, his were far better. "Moving into a new office calls for a celebration?"

"Of course it does. Besides, I want to break in the espresso bar." I crossed over to the machine and stared at my reflection in the polished copper. "Alright, Paige. Let's fire this thing up."

No can do, Captain, she said. *You forked over top of the line dough for this thing, which means it's* vintage. *You're on your own.*

"What?" I said. "You've got to be kidding me! You can't work this hunk of junk?"

Relax, she said. *I can walk you through it. It's not hard. See that pile of white ceramic vessels on the side? Those are called cups.*

"Very funny."

Grab one and place it under one of the four nozzles in front.

I did as Paige instructed. The mover bots rolled out, a bundle of cellophane in hand. The door winked shut behind them.

"Ok," I said. "Now what?"

See that big red button on the side?

I nodded.

Push it.

"You realize this goes against every established color-based button pushing trope, right?"

Don't blame me, said Paige. *This thing's imported.*

Again, I did as she told me. The gleaming contraption started to gurgle.

I noticed Carl smirking. "You find this funny?"

"Sometimes I wonder how the human race ever survived," he said. "Don't get me wrong, I'm glad you did, otherwise I wouldn't be here. But still..."

"Thankfully brewing coffee isn't a crucial survival skill," I said. "Unless it's really early, in which case all bets are off. Either way, I'm sure I'd be capable of sticking a mammoth with a spear if push came to shove."

You just wouldn't be able to light a fire to cook the beast, said Paige with a snicker.

The front door chimes sounded before I could come up with a snappy retort. The mover bots must've forgotten a chassis or something. I'd told them they could come in and out as necessary, but the blasted things insisted on asking for permission every time. "Come in."

The door slid open and in walked a man, tall and broad-shouldered but slim—definitely a non-Cetiean, otherwise his musculature would've been much greater. A crop of short shorn black hair roosted atop his head. Thick eyebrows crowded his brow, contrasting against his carefully manicured designer stubble, all laid over pristine caramel-colored skin. A lightweight ivory jacket draped his shoulders, and he wore a pair of pressed ivory slacks to match. He held a black and white peaked cap under his left arm.

He surveyed me in a single glance. "Richard Weed?"

"I go by Rich." My brows furrowed. "Are you with Jay's? If you want me to fill out a satisfaction survey, you could've sent it via Brain."

That's not a Jay's Relocation uniform... said Paige.

The man stuck out his hand. "Vijay Chatterjee. In-terSTELLA police. I understand you're a private investi-gator?"

I shook it, detecting a hint of cumin and cloves. As I did so, I glanced at my door, which had closed shut be-hind him. As I suspected, nobody had engraved my name and occupation into it during the last few min-utes. "Uh...yes, that's right. How did you find us? To my knowledge our new address isn't in the biz listings yet."

He held his hand toward the plush chairs at the base of my desk. "We have matters to discuss. May we...?"

The espresso machine sputtered and gurgled as it deposited the fruits of its labors to just under the cup's brim. "Right. Yes. Coffee?"

Vijay shook his head. "No, thank you."

He headed toward the chairs, forcing me to follow. I took a seat in my new throne, while Vijay helped him-self to the armchair at my left. Carl seated himself be-side him.

"Well, you've already figured out who *I* am," I said as I settled my cup onto the hardwood. I should've grabbed a saucer, too. "This is my partner Carl."

They shook hands.

"A pleasure." Vijay set his cap down on the desk. "Now let's get to business. I have work to do and little time to spare. I assume, of course, you're familiar with my employer?"

"InterSTELLA?" I said. "You mean the gigantic, multistellar corporation that provides eighty percent of the faster-than-light travel between star systems and keeps the gears of dozens of planetary economies run-

ning with its shipbuilding, cargo, and immigration services? I may have heard of it."

"We're down to about seventy-eight percent," said
Vijay. "Increased competition, you understand."

"Of course," I said. "So what brings you to Cetie?
Correct me if I'm wrong, but if you're with Inter-
STELLA police, you don't have jurisdiction planetside."

Vijay tapped his nose. "Exactly. Which is why I'm
here. I'm looking to engage your services in the capture
of an interstellar brigand."

"You want me to help you capture a *space pirate?*"

"Yes," said Vijay.

I didn't consider myself an expert on body language—limited human contact thanks to droid preva-
lence and a lack of any need to work were to blame—
but as far as I knew, a straight face generally meant
someone *wasn't* joking.

I cleared my throat as I sipped my coffee. "Well, Mr.
Chatterjee, I'm flattered. Really. But tracking down
space pirates isn't what I do."

He leaned in a hair. The man was devilishly handsome, but thanks to extensive prenatal genetic manipu-
lation, who wasn't? "And what exactly *is it* you do, Mr.
Weed?"

The faint whine of the air conditioning system tick-
led my ears as I tried to come up with a fitting yet flattering response.

Vijay settled back into his chair. "That's what I
thought. Look, Mr. Weed—"

"Please," I said. "Rich."

He nodded in acknowledgement. "I'm more familiar
with your tale than you think, Rich. Your business has

dealt largely with trivialities, missing cats and stolen jewelry and the like. Until your last case, that is..."

The massive pile of SEUs I'd received, as well as the contract I'd signed, mandated I keep my silence on the matter. "I'm afraid I don't know what you're talking about."

Vijay didn't look convinced. "I have a GenBorn contact. The Meeks case? He told me everything."

I lifted a brow. Carl gave me a look.

Yes, he knows he can do that better than you can, Paige told me.

Wonderful. "GenBorn told you about Valerie Meeks? They made it very clear they wanted to keep the lid on that."

"It's a good contact," said Vijay. "Besides, this piracy problem is an internal matter for the time being, too. The point is, GenBorn recommended you. Said you waded your way through a difficult investigation with tenacity and poise."

I wasn't sure I believed that. Certainly, I recalled things differently. I thought I'd bumbled my way through the entire encounter and gotten lucky not to die in a fiery explosion.

"I appreciate the praise," I said, "but that doesn't change the fact that I've never tracked down a—what did you call this person? An interstellar brigand? I wouldn't know where to start."

Vijay leaned forward again. "Rich, let me be frank. This...*situation,* should we say, is a big deal, and you won't be the only one on the case. We've dedicated a large portion of our internal resources to investigate it, and we're in the process of recruiting several external teams to assist as well. Your success on the GenBorn case isn't the only reason we've come to you. It's a matter of speed and availability. According to our records, you're the only private investigation service on Cetie, and as you already astutely pointed out, InterSTELLA doesn't have jurisdiction planetside. The opposite is also true. If we want help in space, we have to hire it."

The truth came out. Vijay had come to me because I was available. I felt like the prettiest girl at the dance.

As referrals go, there are worse, said Paige.

I shook my head. "I don't know, Mr. Chatterjee. As I said, I appreciate your interest, but I'm not sure how much help I could be. Deep space isn't my stomping grounds."

"Don't sell yourself short," said Vijay. "Private investigation is about following leads to conclusion, something you've proven yourself capable of. I won't ask you to do anything outside your comfort zone, and you won't be working alone. We'll pair you with a team that compliments your expertise."

A team? I narrowed my eyes.

Carl either mistook my expression, or he knew exactly what was on my mind and cut me off before I had a chance to object. "Rich, if I may..."

"You're always free to speak, Carl."

He intertwined his hands over his lap. "If you'll recall, you've suffered crises of confidence before—"

"Carl!" I said. "Ixnay on the onfidencecay talk-lay, or whatever."

"I don't bring it up to undermine your abilities," said Carl. "I'm merely stating doubt is a common mental state for you. You suffered it on occasion during the

Meeks case, and yet you did, contrary to your own self-deprecating thoughts on the matter—"

Thanks for sharing that with him, Paige...

She gave me a loving virtual nudge.

"—come through victorious, so to speak," said Carl. "In that case, like this one, you wondered if you were up to the task. But have you forgotten why you took up this profession in the first place?"

I knew the reason. It wasn't for the money. I earned more than my fair share of that from the farmland lease bequeathed to me by my grandfather, as well as a much smaller share from my Cetie government work stipend. It also wasn't for the social interaction, even if my last case *had* resulted in an incredibly short-lived fling with a cute-as-a-button professor of exoneurobiology. It was for the challenge, for the thrill of the hunt, for the mental exercise, and to give my life a sense of purpose in my early-middle age.

I met Chatterjee's eyes as I took another sip of my coffee. Dang, the stuff was good.

I think he understood my hesitation. "I can offer a healthy per diem for your services, as well as an exceedingly generous bounty should your efforts lead to the capture of the brigands."

I'd lied a little. Money was *part* of the reason I did what I did. After all, who wouldn't like to take a joyride in their very own Class-A, single capsule, thirty megawatt Iridium™ turbo racer?

"Alright," I said. "If an InterSTELLA rep tells me they're offering good money, I tend to believe them, You've got yourself a detective, Mr. Chatterjee."

Vijay sighed. "Thank goodness. I couldn't afford to waste any more time with indecision."

A message flashed at the corner of my vision, which I immediately saw as originating from V. Chatterjee.

"I've sent you an address," said the man as he rose to his feet. "It's in the orbital spaceport, delta concourse. Pack your bags and meet me there within four galactic standard hour, tops. I'll brief you on everything you need to know once you've gotten to know the rest of your team."

He placed his peaked cap on his head and extended his hand again. I clasped it.

"Looking forward to working with you," he said.

"Likewise." Though I had to admit—I still wasn't sure what I'd committed myself to. I guess that was part of the thrill.

2

A metallic clunk sounded as our climber made initial contact with its port on the bottom of the space elevator. I hung there in my restraints, my posterior hovering a centimeter over my seat as the heavy thumps of clamps and the hiss of airlocks attaching to the exterior of the climber reverberated through the walls.

The last fifteen minutes of the climber ride were always the worst. I was far from a physics whiz, but even I understood the general principles at play. The farther up we went, the weaker the force of gravity pulled us down and the stronger the centrifugal force from our rotation around Cetie pulled us up. As far as I was concerned, the last fifteen minutes or so of the climb I felt weightless—'felt' being the operative term. At that altitude, Cetie still exerted a substantial gravitational pull on me and everything else aboard the climber, but because of the centrifugal force in the opposite direction, it didn't feel that way. And the centrifugal force had nothing to do with the cable anchoring the space elevator to Cetie, as anyone who had ever been aboard a shuttle in geosynchronous orbit could attest to.

A deep, almost subaudible hum emanated from the floor. I sank into the plush cushion underneath me, and my lunch abandoned its attempt to escape from whence it had come. The spaceport's pseudogravity had kicked in—or rather, its power had. The climber had pseudogravity technology onboard, but the energy requirement for the technology was ridiculous. Even if the spaceport operators wanted to appease the stomachs of the folks onboard the climbers, the electrical conductivity of the climber cables couldn't handle it. They'd melt first.

Carl caught the look of relief on my face as he unbuckled his harness. "You sure you're ready? If we go through with this, we'll experience our fair share of stomach-churning microgravity."

Air hissed, a door opened, and people flocked to the exit.

"Have I ever told you I envy you sometimes?" I said.

"I'm serious," said Carl.

"I know. I'll be fine. Honestly, the climber rides are the worst. Fifteen minutes isn't enough time to adjust to the feeling of weightlessness."

We pushed our way through the crowd and into an elevator of the regular variety, which deposited us at the base of the alpha concourse. I'd made the trip to the orbital half of the spaceport enough times not to gape, but it was quite a sight.

The entire alpha concourse was a huge donut, three stories tall and ringed on the sides with thick panes of Pseudaglas. The gleaming curvature of Cetie filled the field of view, most of it a brilliant green from the thick forests that kept the surface temperature of the planet at hospitable levels, mixed with wide swaths of ocean blue and wispy white clouds. A dark curve cut across the side of the world, a line of demarcation caused by Tau Ceti's radiance. Beyond that, I spotted the sparkle of dozens of enormous solar reflectors that mitigated the bleakness of Cetie's long night. They reminded me of stars, but then again, anything that reflected light in outer space did.

Not that I could see any of the view well, mind you. Churning masses of humanity, droids, and aliens of every size, shape, and smell marred my line of sight. Compact, muscular Cetieans milled about amid tall, thin Martians and Spacers and Gains with their universally-accepted perfect proportions. Tall Diraxi with their hard exoskeletons and flickering antennae stood a head above the others, while the Meertori could only be detected by the clank and wheeze of their respirators. Who knows how they saw anything other than bellies from their vantage points. I even spotted an enormous Portloid, clomping around on its wide two-toed feet, impervious as other travelers bounced off its thick grey hide.

With Carl's help, I punched my way out of the morass surrounding the climber station and headed toward the delta concourse, although the alien musk we'd acquired there lingered on our skin. Businesses of all kinds lined the sides of the spaceport, from hotels and eateries to bars and memento shops. All of them featured garish flashing signs, mostly holoprojections rather than physical displays.

Only two and a half weeks had passed since my last trip to the spaceport, but already I found myself getting nostalgic. "I hope Valerie's all right."

Carl gave me a sideways glance. "Please tell me we're not going to that arcade again."

"Arcade?" I asked. "I didn't mention any arcade."

"Please," said Carl. "I know how you think, even when Paige doesn't pass me tidbits. The spaceport brought on thoughts of the Meeks case, which in turn brought you to that moment outside Keelok's Funporium, and the next thing you know we're wasting time and money on that ridiculous overpriced vintage cabinet."

Not to be a stick in the mud, said Paige, *but time is the more important factor here. Rich, you could've been more judicious in packing your overnight bag.*

"We'll make it in time," I said, "mostly because I have no intention of dropping by Keelok's. Seriously, Carl, that wasn't what I was thinking. I was...*reminiscing.*"

He gave me a cheeky smirk. "The one that got away, huh?"

I snorted. "Don't be like that. You know I never pined after Valerie. Professor Castaneva on the other hand..."

"Yeah, about her," said Carl. "Sorry that petered out so quickly."

I shrugged. "She wasn't interested in me. She was into the thrill of being with a real life private detective."

At least she helped you end your dry streak, said Paige.

I cringed. "Can we please not call it that? When you use the word 'streak,' you make it sound as if I was counting the days."

Maybe you weren't, said Paige. *Carl and I were.*

I glanced at my partner.

He shrugged. "To be fair, it's not really counting with an AI. We remember everything without giving it conscious thought."

I shut my yapper, mostly because I didn't want to go into my sexual escapades with Carl and Paige. Not that I had any choice with Paige. She was always there, even in the heat of the moment, so to speak.

A cylindrical aquarium surrounded the motorized walkway to the delta concourse. Fishes of a thousand different colors, eels, jellyfish, manta rays, cuttlefish, and sharks, with schools of lampreys and other opportunists latched to their fins, swam over and under and around us as we walked on the moving carpets. The sheer audacity of transporting so much water—never mind the wildlife—up to the spaceport for a mere visual display boggled the mind. It also explained why climber tickets and docking fees were so danged expensive.

As the walkway spit us into the food court at the base of the delta concourse, I double checked the address Vijay had sent. The text flashed at the lower right of my vision. *Concourse delta, second level, C wing, dock 139.* When I'd first read it, I'd been surprised Vijay had instructed us to meet at a dock. Rather, I'd expected we'd meet at the InterSTELLA police headquarters aboard the spaceport. Paige, of course, had chided me mercilessly over that assumption, mostly because Vijay had instructed me to pack my bags, to which I'd replied we could've met at the spaceport and *then* left on a longer journey afterwards. We'd gone back and forth for a while, during which I'm sure I'd seemed a maniac to third parties, but I wasn't the only one who argued with his Brain. Not that anyone cared. Thanks to fully-immersive Brain games and digital experiences, most folks were too introverted to care a whit about anyone else's goings on. Honestly, the only place where humans and aliens regularly outnumbered droids was at sporting events and the spaceport.

I took a quick glance around the food court, but all I could see were flashing holodisplays for sushi, pizza, and a hay-like Tak delicacy known as Snurl. "Paige...a little help?"

Elevator on your right, she said. *Take it to the second floor and hang a left. Even you should be able to figure it out from there.*

I followed her instructions, and the elevator doors closed behind me with a puff.

You know, Rich, there's something I've been meaning to tell you.

"Yes?" A rush of acceleration hit me from the elevator.

Well, it's more of a reminder, really, Paige said. *My servenets are located in Pylon Alpha. The further away we travel, the longer it'll take me to relay information back and forth.*

"That pesky speed of light," I said.

Yeah, physics is a real drag. The point is, you may not be able to count on me quite as much as you normally do during this pirate hunting endeavor.

I blinked as the elevator door reopened. "I thought you stored your digital intelligence imprint locally on my Brain."

"I think what Paige is getting at," said Carl, "is she won't be able to access information quickly."

Precisely, said Paige. *Don't worry, Rich. I'll be as present and vivacious as ever. And I'll remember to flush the toilet for you if you forget how. But if you task me with any complex search queries or statistical analyses, I'll have to offload them to the main servenet, and that'll take a bit more time than you're used to.*

"Got it," I said. "But this could be a good test. Instead of relying solely on you, I'll get to test my own gray matter. We'll see how good of an investigator I really am."

The utter silence Carl and Paige responded with was very reassuring.

I found Vijay sitting outside the airlock for dock one thirty-nine. His eyes had a glassy look to them, and I figured he was busy responding to Brain missives, familiarizing himself with the latest InterSTELLA reports, or watching alien pornography. He must've had his Brain set to alert him in the event of external stimuli, as after a moment he blinked, glanced at me, and stood.

"There you are." He glanced at my lightweight guayabera and slacks. "Is...that what you're wearing?"

"It's detective attire," I said. "It's traditional."

Neither of those statements were necessarily true. The inspiration for my wardrobe had come from old PI vid-docs and novels. In those, the protagonists always wore heavy trench coats and hats, but none of them lived on planets where mid-afternoon temperatures routinely exceeded 40°C. I'd compromised.

Vijay shrugged. "I would've picked something that doesn't flair up at the waist in zero gravity, but your call. Are you ready to go?"

"I will be as soon as my bag arrives," I said.

"I'll ping the central delivery service," said Vijay. "In the meantime, we'll board. That way we can leave as soon as possible."

The uniformed man crossed to a panel on the wall. He pressed his thumb against the reader at the bottom and his eye to the reader at the top. After confirming his identity, the door to his left hissed.

"So," I said as the airlock progressed through its cycles. "Care to share any more information about where we're going and how I'm supposed to tackle this case?"

"Your debriefing will occur on the *Snowbell*," said Vijay. "That's where you'll meet the last of your team. And before you ask, I'm waiting because I'd rather not have to explain everything twice. Also because some of the information you'll receive is classified and the *Snowbell* is secure."

"The *Snowbell*?" I asked.

Vijay blinked, his face impassive. "All InterSTELLA ships are named after flowers."

I pursed my lips. I was getting the impression Vijay wasn't much of a people person. Then again, perhaps he was under a lot of stress. Pirate attacks could do that to a man—I assumed.

The airlock door opened with a puff. "And I don't suppose this is the *Snowbell*?"

Chatterjee shook his head. "This is a small transport vessel. The *Snowbell* is one of our mobile operations vessels and the host of my current assignment. It's several hours farther out in orbit." He held his hand out. "After you."

A *small transport vessel?* That meant no pseudogravity. I tried to curb my enthusiasm as I stepped into the airlock.

3

Carl followed me, and Vijay entered last. The doors shut behind him, and the rumbling pump cycle began anew. As the pumps groaned and whirred, the pseudogravity abruptly shut off. I floated lazily toward the ceiling, and my lunch rose toward my throat in a manner I would describe as anything *but* lazy.

Vijay gave me a sidelong look. "You...travel much?"

"Don't worry about me. I'll be—huurgh!—fine. It's the first fifteen minutes or so that are—hurgh—tough."

Vijay didn't respond, but he gave his pristine white uniform a glance. That made it pretty clear where his priorities lay.

The door to the transport vessel slid open with a hiss. I grabbed a handle at its side and pulled myself through, upon which I found myself barreling straight toward the chest of a woman in a deep purple jumpsuit.

I held out my hands and started to mumble apologies. "Sorry. My bad. I—"

Her hand darted out and grabbed me by the wrist. She pivoted and pulled, and my body swung wildly. The vessel's cabin spun around me in a blur, and a second later I landed lightly on my feet, right-side up—or so I decided given the multi-directional functionality of my surroundings.

I blinked and focused on the woman as she released my wrist. To my eyes, she seemed impossibly tall— almost two meters in height—and slender enough that a pleasant vacation on a Cetie beach would've felt to her like being slowly crushed under a boulder. Her skin was as pale as eggshell, and her hair, cut into a sharp inverted bob, gleamed a brilliant, platinum blonde. Though she possessed an undeniable beauty, it was a severe form. Everything about her, from her nose to her cheek bones to her chin, was angular and sharp. Between that, her lithe form, and her quick reflexes, I got the impression she could spear me on her index finger if she so desired.

After looking me over with poorly hidden contempt, she called over her shoulder. "This is the guy?"

Vijay followed me through the hatch. "This is him."

The woman frowned. "He looks green."

"Huurgh! I'll be fine. Promise." Although I wasn't so sure anymore. That bit of wrist gymnastics hadn't helped any.

"I meant green as in raw. Inexperienced." She glanced back at Vijay. "He can't even float properly. He's supposed to help us track down a pirate boss how exactly?"

Despite my disorientation, it didn't fly over my head that she'd yet to address me directly. No matter. I could be the bigger man. Heck, I probably had forty kilos on her.

"Thanks for the assist, by the way. The name's Rich Weed, private investigator at large. That droid over there is my pal Carl." He'd entered through the hatch. "You are?"

The woman eyed me, snorted, and shook her head. To Vijay: "I'm going back to my ship. See you aboard the *Snowbell.*"

She clambered through the open hatch, disappearing as the airlock closed behind her.

Well, she seems lovely, said Paige.

I turned to Vijay, my hand gripping a protrusion on the wall to keep myself from spinning. "I hesitate to ask, but who was that?"

"Tarja Olli. Bounty hunter," he said.

"And let me guess—"

Vijay nodded preemptively. "She's part of your team. Don't worry, I'm sure you'll get along swimmingly. Word on the spaceport is she's excellent at her job."

"What does that have to do with us getting along?" I asked.

"Go ahead and get yourself strapped in," said Vijay. "We'll be departing soon. Cruising acceleration is just under Cetie's gravitation pull, so you should feel right at home during the trip."

Vijay was proving himself a master of the non-answer. He pushed off toward the cockpit, leaving me to figure out where to situate myself.

I took a look around. For a transport shuttle, it wasn't too shabby. I had room to stretch my arms and wiggle my toes. Two rows of four seats were set into opposing walls, each of them equipped with a four point harness and generous cushions in the event the shuttle needed to crank up the g's. Each wall also featured a thin, oblong window. Through one I could see nothing more than the spaceport's shiny bulwark, but through the other I caught another glimpse of Cetie's earth-toned majesty. Above that second window I found an inscription, brightly lit in iridescent paint:

InterSTELLA
Titans in Transport since 2312

I pushed off the ceiling and managed to get close enough to one of the seats to grab hold of the straps. From there it was a simple matter of flailing about wildly and almost ralphing over the seat cushions before I managed to hook both of my shoulders under the harness.

Carl floated over gently as I fastened the buckles on my restraints, sliding into the seat beside me with a practiced ease.

"Don't gloat," I told him.

"I wasn't about to," he said. "You shouldn't be embarrassed. There's a perfectly good reason why I'm so adept in microgravity and you're not."

"Does it have to do with gastrointestinal juices and that little thingy in my inner ear?"

"Muscle memory," said Carl. "Or lack thereof. If you don't practice a physical task on a regular basis, you lose your proficiency. I don't."

Basically, Carl's saying he could kick your ass in zero g kung-fu, said Paige.

I snorted. "Not mine. He's subliminally programmed to adore me, whether he likes it or not. I doubt he could lift a finger against me if he tried."

Carl's face fell ever so slightly, an action made possible only by the state of the art expressions upgrade he'd undergone back before my time. It was a blessing and a curse—a blessing in the sense that his reactions were indistinguishable from those of a real human, but a curse in that said expressions were hardwired into him so that he couldn't avoid them even if he wanted to. That, in turn, was another blessing—for me. I cared for Carl, and I didn't want to hurt his feelings. I simply tended to forget the things that triggered him—like any mention of his incomplete free will.

I nodded to the logo on the wall to change the subject. "Any idea what InterSTELLA stands for? I've always been curious."

Nothing, actually, said Paige before Carl could chime in.

"Really?" I said. "I always assumed it was a complicated acronym."

It was, said Paige. *Originally it stood for Science-, Technology-, and Engineering-based Lightspeed reLocation Associates, but about two hundred years after their founding, they perfected their Alcubierre drive technology, and the Lightspeed part became obsolete. They couldn't come up with another name that fit the acronym, and their brand was pretty well established at that point, so they scrapped the underlying meaning altogether and went with InterSTELLA.*

I nodded to my partner. "Did you know that?"

"I don't know everything, Rich," he said. "You'll have to remember that as we travel. I'll be as limited as Paige in my understanding of the universe while in deep space."

"But you knew that bit about InterSTELLA, didn't you?"

"I did."

"Of course."

An unfamiliar voice crackled in the back of my mind, at least unfamiliar in the sense that I hadn't received a Brain call from him yet.

Rich? Vijay. Your bags made it aboard. You set for liftoff?

Paige must've patched him through without my knowledge. It made sense to have a direct line of contact with him for the time being, though. *Ready when you are. Let's get some weight on this baby.*

Alright. Here we go then, he said.

I heard a pair of thumps and felt a jostle as the spaceport's clamps released us. A feather-light touch pushed me against the back of my chair. When I looked over my shoulder, I saw the smooth walls of the spaceport slowly recede.

Another feather light touch pushed me sideways, but I might not have even noticed it if not for the shift of Cetie's profile in relation to the window across from me.

I floated, pushed ever so slightly back and to the sides for about a minute before another communication came from Vijay.

Ready for thrust.

Soundlessly, the shuttle's resonant cavity thrusters kicked in, pushing me against the bottom of my seat cushion and restoring my weight. Like most planetary transport vessels, the shuttle had been designed to fly along a trajectory at a constant linear acceleration, in this case at a level somewhere between Earth and Cetie's gravitational pulls, until the halfway mark of the journey, at which point the shuttle would rotate a hundred and eighty degrees and decelerate at the same rate. Barring use of the Alcubierre drive, which was frowned upon within solar systems, it was the fastest way to get around, and it allowed for interior constructions of spaceships that more or less resembled planetside dwellings.

How long until our rendezvous with the Snowbell? I asked Vijay via Brain.

Three standard galactic hours, give or take five minutes, he responded.

I unbuckled my restraints and stood. Three hours would be more than enough time to enjoy a holovid or two, which I'd be happy to do if I could only find something to munch on first. Hopefully that wouldn't prove to be a problem. Vijay hadn't warned me to pack my own snacks.

4

I stood in an airlock on the *Snowbell*, listening to the rhythm of the pumps and feeling the light breeze of whistling air on my face when the ship's pseudogravity kicked in.

"Oh yeah. That's the ticket," I said as my feet settled against the floor.

Carl gave me a dubious glance. "You know, I'm well aware I can never fully understand your negative reaction to microgravity given I don't suffer the same physiological response as you, but is it really that bad? We were under the equivalent of one point six g's the entire trip over, barring the turn. You act as if you haven't felt solid ground underfoot for a month."

"As I've already mentioned, it's the transition that's problematic," I said. "And I agree with you one hundred percent. You *can't* ever know what it feels like to almost lose your lunch and have your heart jump into your throat. It's a horrible feeling, one nobody can fully acclimate to no matter how many times they go through it."

"Mr. Chatterjee doesn't seem to be suffering any ill effects."

Carl pointed him out. He stood with us in the airlock, his caramel-colored complexion looking no paler than normal, but his face betrayed something else. Impatience or uneasiness perhaps, but not from gastrointestinal distress. Rather, I got the impression he was claustrophobic. Either that or he didn't care for my company. He certainly hadn't engaged me in conversation during our trip over.

Could be he's an Intro, said Paige.

In his line of work? I said. *Doubtful. Unless he's a desk jockey who's been plucked from his castle to take part in a recruiting expedition he has no interest in.*

Actually, that sounds plausible, said Paige.

And you doubted my deductive reasoning, I chided her.

Carl continued to look at me, expecting an answer, but I gave him none. Hey, if the truth portrayed me in a less than glamorous light, I knew when to keep my mouth shut.

The interior airlock door opened, and Chatterjee waved us forward. "Follow me."

I stepped into a sterile, white-paneled hallway. According to the signage, we'd arrived at dock P7. Apparently the *Snowbell* was a big girl. Big enough for pseudogravity, anyway.

My footfalls made satisfying thumps as we walked after our uniformed commander-in-chief. "You know, Carl, I know you might think I complain too much, but it's visionaries like me who effect change."

He gave me a superbly lifted eyebrow. "Where are you going with this?"

"Pseudogravity," I said. "I don't like how it's limited to ships with larger masses and with fusion reactors that can produce ridiculous amounts of power. I want it on every ship, from the largest freighter to the smallest fighter. I make my thoughts known, as do other like minded individuals, and though the power of the free market, we effect change."

"You can't be serious," said Carl. "For one thing, the volume of your complaining has nothing to do with the purchasing power of your bank account. For another, moaning won't change the physical limitations of pseudogravity. It can't be implemented on smaller crafts. It's not possible."

"Please," I said. "You and I both know that's a load of Tak dung. All kinds of things are physically possible that we don't believe to be. If humanity had appeased itself with the physically likely, we'd still be scooting around at sub-light speed on rotating centrifuges powered by radioactive sludge and firing propellant out our—AHH!"

I screeched to a halt as we turned a corner, my face almost slamming into the slight, purple Spandette-clad bosom of Tarja Olli.

"What the...? What are you doing here?" I asked.

She glanced at Vijay, who'd barely slowed. "Is he serious?"

I'd tried a gentlemanly approach upon first introduction, but that hadn't worked, and my patience grew thinner with each of Tarja's nose-upturned remarks.

"I'm right here you know. And what I meant was, how'd you beat us to the *Snowbell*?"

She dropped into step alongside Vijay and talked to me over her shoulder. "How fast were you going?"

"We pulled about one point six—"

"It was a rhetorical question," said Tarja. "I went faster than that and met you here, obviously."

I snorted. "Really? *You*?"

She regarded me with cool eyes. "Let me guess. You think a tall, skinny Spacer like me can't handle multiple g's. I'm a frail flower that'll break under the slightest breeze."

"Flowers aren't usually as tall as you are," I said. "Plus they're pleasing to the senses. You're more like a twig embrittled by dry rot."

Tarja sniffed and turned her gaze back down the hall. "Well, at least he's got spine."

"Yes," I said. "A stout one that won't break under pressure."

"The metaphor's spent, hoss," said Tarja. "Give it up."

I clenched my teeth and glanced at Carl. He shrugged in response. He wasn't good at conflict. It wasn't in his subroutines.

Far be it from me to meddle in a blossoming relationship, said Paige, *but you do remember what you signed up for, right? You're going to have to work with this woman whether you like it or not. Might not hurt to put your best foot forward.*

I sputtered a little. *My best foot? I didn't start this fire.*

You haven't lifted a finger to put it out either, said Paige. *You seem intent on adding oxidizers to the flames.*

Tarja proceeded, oblivious to my internal monologue. "So, Vijay, are you going to explain the situation with these pirates or what?"

"Once we reach my office and you meet Ducic, yes," he said. "I pinged him. He'll meet us there."

Honestly, I'd started to wonder about Chatterjee's steel trap-like jaw myself. He'd claimed he didn't want to explain himself more than once. I supposed that was possible, but we'd spent several hours together aboard the shuttle and the man hadn't uttered more than a couple words to me. Even for an Intro, he seemed particularly intent on avoiding conversation.

We followed Vijay through sterile corridors and a largely empty mess hall, passing the occasional Inter-STELLA employee, some dressed in white police garb and others dressed in the traditional company navy blue. Engineers and scientists and maintenance crew, most likely. Some gave Chatterjee an approving head nod while others passed us by with nary a glance.

A door winked open in front of Vijay, and I followed him and Tarja through the gap.

The office within was cozy to say the least. Vijay skirted around a thin, molded plastic desk and pointed to a pair of stools on the other side. A holoprojector poked out from between the lights on the ceiling, and a large interactive display covered the right hand wall. The opposite wall featured built in shelving and cabinets, the free space of which was occupied by Vijay's personal effects: a photo projection of him with a dark haired woman and a scruffy-haired boy, a pair of framed golden service medals with InterSTELLA's logo wrapped around the edges, and a worn cricket bat with a wide signature scrawled across the front in indelible ink.

In front of all that, filling almost half the office and blocking my access to the stools, stood a droopy-eyed Tak.

The Taks were an interesting race—quadrupedal and beefy, with long torsos and undersized, rudimentary hands at the front of their bodies, almost as if they were the product of a horribly conceived gene splicing experiment between humans, rhinos, and giraffes. Their heads, however, were one hundred percent cow. Exobiologists would disagree, I'm sure, citing the flatness of their brows or the width of their nostrils, but to any independent observer like me, the only thing separating them from complete and total bovineness was their lack of ink spots.

As often as not they walked around naked, but this particular Tak wore a navy lab coat with a bright Inter-STELLA insignia over the right breast pocket. He—She? It? Their gender was less obvious than our own—eyed me with disinterest. Or perhaps contempt. Or maybe he was drowsy. I couldn't read Tak body language very well.

Vijay waved to the two stools. "Go on. Have a seat."

Tarja helped herself to the stool by the display, leaving me the seat by the Tak. Carl didn't have muscles to rest, so it was mine for the taking, but it would be a tight fit. I'd have to press half my body against the beast's flank, never mind how I'd have to contort myself to get there in the first place.

The Tak noticed my hesitation. "Does my presence impede you, human? I am capable of rearrangement if necessity exits."

Even with universal Brain translation, Tak speech had a way of coming across as less than transparent. Something about the way our minds processed language and grammar didn't quite jive.

"No, don't worry about it," I said. "I'll be fine right here. Spare elbow room and all that." The door blinked shut behind me, clipping me on the rear.

"Suit yourself," said Vijay. "Tarja. Rich. Meet the final member of your team, Ducic. He's with our interplanetary physics division. Ducic—Tarja Olli and Rich Weed."

"Really?" I said with a lift of my brow. "Him?"

Ducic shifted his snout. "I must inform you I am familiar with human expressive systems. Your passive expression of doubt has not gone unnoticed. If the underlying incertitude of your emotion stems from my race, I would point you in the direction of InterSTELLA workplace equality manual, chapter forty-four, section C. If said derision stems from my species' ability to conduct physics, that is perhaps a more egregious slight."

Tarja turned her head toward me, her cool eyes holding a twinkle of mirth. "You really need to pull that foot out of your mouth, tank."

"The name's Rich," I said. "Not tank or hoss or beefcake or whatever else you think is appropriate. My muscle tone is a gravitational side-effect. You got a problem with it?"

She smiled at me. "You'd rather I call you shorty?"

"Excellent," said Vijay. "Introductions are flying all around...alongside other things. Now if you don't mind, please SHUT UP and listen so I can brief you on the mission parameters!"

Vijay's cheeks had darkened, and his face showed signs of strain. I'd already caught a glimpse of the mountain on his shoulders, slowly crushing him under its pressure. I'd also guessed at his introversion. If I was right about it, having a quartet of humans, aliens, and droids in his office wasn't helping his hormone levels. Add to that my and everyone else's inability to conduct ourselves in a professional manner, and I'd argue his outburst was warranted.

"Sorry. I—we—shouldn't have acted that way." I eyed Tarja and Ducic to see if they agreed, but the bounty hunter had her back to me and I couldn't get a bead on the Tak because, well...cow face. "Let's talk pirates."

5

"Before I start," said Vijay, "let me preface this discussion by saying none of the following information is to travel outside InterSTELLA hulls. That isn't to say you can't talk about it with anyone, but you need to make sure discussion takes place with individuals who've been granted proper clearance. Ducic's level has been elevated for this precise purpose. He'll be able to guide you on who you can and can't talk to, among other things.

"Now. Tarja. Rich." He gave each of us a bob of his head. "You've been brought on to help track down a group of interstellar thieves who've made several attacks upon our transports."

The display at the side of the room sprang to life, showing a rendition of the Tau Ceti system on the bottom right, complete with the inhabited planets Cetie and Cetif, the lifeless b-d husks, and the asteroid belt. The top left of the display showed the Sol system, which I deduced from my knowledge of planetary geography as well as the informative lettering present on the screen.

"All the attacks thus far have occurred along the Sol-Tau Ceti corridor," said Vijay. "Five ships in total have been targeted. The *Jimsonweed*, the *Libertia*, the *Kalanchoe*, the *Butterwort*, and the *Agapetes*."

The ships, along with their names and classifications, appeared on the display, each with a trajectory showing their path from Sol to Tau Ceti or vice versa.

"For your knowledge," said Ducic, "said display is not to correct scale."

How did Taks express sarcasm? Hopefully it was with the dopey, lowered-chin expression the alien now gave me. "Yeah, I got that. Thanks."

Vijay continued. "So far, the heists have followed a fairly predictable pattern. Two attacks, in relatively quick succession, followed by a long*er*, if not necessarily long, period of inactivity. Because of this, you can imagine we're on high alert for the sixth attack."

"What have the pirates stolen?" asked Tarja.

The holoprojector whirred into action, displaying each of the vessels in three dimensions in the air in front of us.

"All of the ships are freighters," said Vijay. "Limited crew quarters, with large unpressurized hulls for raw materials. In all cases, those materials have been heavy metals. Silver, palladium, tungsten, and iridium."

"That's all the pirates have stolen?" Tarja asked. "They didn't take any weapons or tech or luxury goods?"

Vijay nodded. "Correct."

"And they haven't taken any hostages or made any demands?" asked Tarja.

Vijay shook his head.

I eyed the display, which I'd been perfectly aware was not to scale, thank you very much, Ducic. "You mentioned the attacks have occurred along the Sol-Tau Ceti corridor. I'm no expert on interstellar transportation, but isn't that one of the most heavily traveled lines in the galaxy? At least for us humans? How is it whoever's attacking these ships has eluded capture five times now?"

"Good question," said Vijay. "It's why this has remained an internal matter. It's also why Ducic is part of your team. Care to explain the circumstances to your new compatriots?"

The Tak flapped his gums as he talked, flashing me a glimpse of his creepy square-toothed smile. "By best held knowledge of our collective intelligences, said pirate attacks appear to have occurred while freighters have been contained within the solitary embrace of their warp bubbles."

I blinked. "Come again?"

"Are your knowledge receptors familiar with the Alcubierre drive, human?"

"The warp engine that facilitates faster-than-light travel between star systems?" I said. "Yes, I'm familiar with it."

"You have bypassed crux of my query," said Ducic. "Are you familiar with its function? Down to the level of testicles and lightning?"

"Uh...*what?*"

I think he means 'nuts and bolts,' said Paige. *Taks are notoriously poor at grasping idioms.*

Ducic took my response as a negative. "How can I express this in prone man's terms? Alcubierre drive function is driven by compression and expansion of space time. A vessel equipped with said engine does not move by mechanics of thrust. It moves not at all. Space time bends around it. Barrier created between compressed or stretched space time and space at pristine elasticity is informally dubbed the warp bubble."

I'd known that already. If I hadn't, Ducic's broken explanation wouldn't have enlightened me. "Let me get this straight. You're saying pirates are attacking your ships while they're *in* the warp bubble? How?"

Ducic's ears flattened.

Paige came to my rescue. *That's his equivalent of a shrug.*

"So these pirates are dropping in on your freighters mid-warp, and you have no idea how they might be doing it?"

Ducic nodded. At least that expression crossed interspecies boundaries.

"Is that even possible?" I asked.

"Theoretically, yes," said Vijay. "Practically, no—or so we thought. Our suspicion is they have advanced tech that grants them superior tactical advantages. We're still working out the details."

I tried to wrap my head around that. Pirates? With Alcubierre drive technology that beat the pants off what InterSTELLA had? How could that be?

Vijay didn't afford me time to think. "It gets more complicated, I'm afraid. I've told you each attack occurred along the Sol-Tau Ceti corridor, and I meant that quite literally. The attacks took place at warp speed in deep space. But here's the thing about Alcubierre drive technology. It's a straight shot sort of deal. You can't change trajectory mid-warp."

"Engine parameters are set prior to engagement," said Ducic. "Length of drive action and trajectory. Engage, fly, arrive. Slice of pie."

"Yeah," said Tarja. "I'm sure it's a cakewalk."

"All of which means a ship attacking another along the Sol-Tau Ceti line must be on the same trajectory," said Vijay. "The starting and ending points could be dissimilar if different engine burn lengths were inputted, so the pirates didn't necessarily originate in the Sol or Tau Ceti systems, but we do have a set of linear coordinates along which the brigands must've exited warp."

"Where are you going with this?" I asked.

"Compression and expansion of space time is highly energetic process," said Ducic. "Surely you must wonder why Alcubierre drive use is prohibited near populated structures? Particles gathered in warp bubble accumulate during transit, then are emitted in shockwave upon arrival. Like sonic bang. Spread of blast is more contained now than in early engine models, but still nasty."

"And?" I said.

"Those energetic particles can be sensed," said Vijay. "They have very specific energies. Clusters of energetic particles like that don't normally exist on their own in deep space."

"So you've been sending recon teams to search for warp exit signatures," said Tarja. "Let me guess. You haven't found any."

Vijay shook his head. "We've had teams of scout ships dropping in and out all over the Sol-Tau Ceti corridor, sweeping the area for energetic particle signatures. Ditto for spots along that same line extending past Sol and Tau Ceti. Problem is that's a hell of a lot of empty space. They've yet to find anything."

"Should particles be found," said Ducic, "not only would it reveal where pirates ceased drive operation, but exit signatures could be used to trace new outbound trajectory. Not useful if pirates are heading to random spot in deep space, but effective in trying to find planetary hideouts."

"So to recap," I said, "you've got a team of space thieves dropping on your ships in mid-warp. You don't know where they've originated from or where they're going, and all evidence points to them not being able to do the very thing they're doing in the first place."

Ducic nodded again. "If I possessed opposable thumbs, I would thumb my snout at you, human."

I frowned, but Paige stopped me before I said anything. *He doesn't actually mean thumb. It's not an insult. He's trying to say you're right.*

Tarja snorted. "Fabulous. I hope you've got *something* for us to go on, otherwise we're liable to sit around warming our chairs while we collect our per diems— which is fine by me, but I suspect you had higher hopes when you brought us on board."

"We did catch a break," said Vijay. "We recovered physical evidence of the pirates from their most recent assault on the *Agapetes*, and we have extensive surveillance footage from each of the five attacks."

The holoprojected ships blinked out of existence, and the display faded to black.

"Ducic will be your contact from here on out," continued Vijay. "He's familiar with the parameters of the attacks, and he's been granted access to all data files, individuals, and pieces of physical evidence you might need to continue your investigation. I'm sure you have more questions, but you'll have to defer to him. If something stumps him, he can message me via Brain, but only as a last recourse. As you can imagine, this situation has burdened me with a heavy load in *addition* to my regular work, and as an InterSTELLA police official, I have to attack it from multiple angles. Now, Ducic? If you would?"

Vijay delivered the last half of his speech with glazed eyes that made me think he hadn't even waited to finish talking before he delved into his backlog of Brain missives.

The Tak physicist gave us a nod. "Humans and android. Please, if you would follow?"

6

I exited the office first, not as an affront to Ducic's authority but because I didn't want to have my pelvis crushed between his beefy, roughage-thickened flank and the room's molded plastic desk. Carl and Tarja joined me.

As I waited for Ducic to amble around the tight corner, I spared another glance Chatterjee's way. The man had totally checked out. Based on his likely personality type, I could understand his unease with us all in his presence, but the man had gone out of his way to recruit both myself and Tarja. I distinctly remembered his relief when I'd agree to take part in the investigation, so it struck me as odd the level of nonchalance with which he passed us off into Ducic's tutelage.

Ducic set off down the hallway, his hooves clacking against the floor as he walked. "This way, please."

Tarja pushed past me to settle herself at the Tak's side, affording me not even so much as a glance as she did so. I'd wager the woman would knock her own grandmother to the floor for an advantage.

"So, Ducic..." she said. "Vijay mentioned evidence? What exactly did the pirates leave behind? Something we can use to track them?"

"Your suspicions are stain on," said Ducic. "That most recently expressed hope is ours as well. Said pirates certainly did not mean to leave as much as they did. Not unless they and their brethren are members of a cult of ruination."

Tarja adopted a mask of confusion. "Come again?"

I wiped a similar look from my face. "Look, Ducic, I know you probably don't do it intentionally, but could you try to be less opaque?"

Ducic shook his head. "You must be unfamiliar with my anatomy, human. Voluntary translucency is not physiologically possible for me. I am not even capable of modifying my skin pigmentation."

"Just try to make a little more sense," I said. "And stop calling me 'human.' The name's Rich. Use it."

"Apologies...*Rich*," said Ducic. "It is not my intent to be obfuscatory. I will attempt to explain. Most recent pirate encounter occurred aboard the *Agapetes*. Crew of said freighter, as crew of all ships with cargos of interest to the attacking marauders, had been informed of risk. Where increased crew and guards had been possible to be implemented, they were, but many Inter-STELLA freighters are not designed for said tasks. Ships are large, but crew quarters and life support systems are not. Metaphorically speaking, in case of the last. Life support systems, even on transports, occupy a large fraction of ship's mass and volume. But I think I—how would say? Am straying?—from the topic.

"Crux of my tale is defenses aboard vessels have been increased, but sadly not aboard the *Agapetes*. Whether by knowledge or chance, pirates attacked ship. Not to imply crew was not prepared for the possibility. A clever mechanist—machinist? engineer?—subverted ship safety systems during said attack. A hatch adjacent to cargo hold was opened, and several pirates lost to the void of space. One more was caught under netting in cargo hold, though also killed by violence of pressure loss. His fellow thieves thought him lost to warp bubble and did not try to recover him. He was, in fact, not even discovered until crew went to investigate damage to hold. Quite a fortuitous turn of events, one must admit. I believe this is, how you would say, plucking a shot fish from a cask?"

"Not even close," I said.

Come on, said Paige. *You've got to give him credit for trying.*

"So you've got one of the pirate's bodies?" asked Tarja.

"As well as his tools and personal belongings," said Ducic. "All were linked to him via tethers."

"Of course they were," said Tarja. "These are pirates we're dealing with, not moronic flatlanders."

"As a flatlander, I resent that," I said.

"But not as a moron?" said Tarja.

I recalled Paige's advice and swallowed back an insult. "You know, I think I'm developing a pretty good idea of why you work alone." That got me a snort in response. "So where's the body, Ducic?"

"Here, on the *Snowbell*," he said. "In our medical bay. We have cryogenic stasis pods available for emergency circumstances. If medical prowess of our team is insufficient to cure an individual of their ailment, we can store them for transport to more advanced facilities. They also provide ideal storage for deceased. Olfactory problems otherwise persist."

We stepped back into the mess hall, but rather than head toward the docking bays, we hooked a right and found a lift. The doors slid open as we approached, and upon Ducic's spoken command, it whisked us down a couple levels.

When it spit us out, I found myself staring at a pair of doorways, one marked in red and white diagonal stripes and with 'MEDICAL' imprinted across the front seam, and the other with a more garish horizontal yellow stripe and 'BRIG' in bold, black letters.

I glanced at the door to the prisoner cells before following Ducic through the opposite opening. "I don't suppose you've been lucky enough to take any of the pirates alive, have you?"

"If so," said Ducic, "would you not suppose I would have shared said piece of information upon first introduction?"

I found the medical bay even more white and pristine than the rest of the ship. Thin white cots extended from the wall on retractable bases, each immaculately made and adorned with pillows that looked as if they'd never been used. Full body imagers hung from the ceiling, curved panels that resembled solar mirrors except for the complicated array of sensors within. Slips containing adhesive-backed biometric sensors, each thinner than a piece of paper, filled the alcoves at the side of each bed. Hoses for oxygen hung on the walls alongside handheld medical scanners and more archaic tools like otoscopes. I didn't see any cutting or stabbing implements, so I assumed those were locked up in the cabinets on the far side.

Across from the row of neatly made beds, I spotted a couple of longer cots flanked by something that resembled a gigantic pair of pliers. Next to those were a pair of open-fronted stalls, each of them wide enough for a horse but fitted with an array of tools and displays that would've been excessive even for the most fervent of racehorse breeders. Unlike most ships of human construction, the med bay aboard the *Snowbell* was equipped to deal with an array of different species. For Ducic's sake, I hoped the level of technical expertise of the medical staff matched the equipment.

All the cots and stalls were empty, but a doctor in a white coat sat in a chair against the far wall. He gave a nod to Ducic as we passed through the medical bay and into a smaller chamber within.

The skin on my arms prickled as we entered, and I suppressed a shiver. Two rows of a half-dozen cryogenic storage tubes rested against opposite walls, facing each other like frosty, silent sentinels. The hiss of forced air cycling through a vent mixed with the low hum of the cryo pods' compression pumps.

A Dirax, roughly two meters ten tall and wearing only a lime green vest over its chest, stood in front of the pod against the far wall. Its carapace gleamed in the muted, blue-tinted lighting. Though the creature's armor-plated arms hung low at its sides, its antennae flicked rapidly in sharp, targeted bursts as it interacted with the display on the front of the cryo pod. The Diraxi's unique cranial architecture enabled them to network with any wirelessly enabled digital technology through thought alone, much like anyone equipped with Brain technology could. Scientists referred to the ability as electromagnetic speech, but the common definition of telepathy was equally valid.

Our crew approached the large insectoid. Ducic broke the ice. "Dirax. A word, if you please."

Because of their evolved electromagnetically-based communications, the Diraxi had no auditory sensory organs to speak of. Ducic must've instructed his Tak-optimized Brain to repeat his speech to the Diraxi electronically, as I also did. Though some people managed it, I found it odd to conduct in-person conversations entirely via Brain.

The tall alien neglected to turn to face us, but its speech appeared in my mind, much as Paige's own banter would. *Ducic. You bring guests. Am I to assume these are the additional members of your investigative team?*

"Correct," said Ducic. "If I may? This tall one is named Tarja Olli. We are to assume she is a hunter of bounties of the living and piratical variety."

"You are to assume correctly," she said with a tip of her chin.

"And this other is named Rich Weed. He is some sort of investigative professional. Based on search queries, his qualifications seem dubious at best. The droid is in Rich's charge. I have yet to be introduced. He is exceptionally quiet, and if I were prone to assumptions, I would categorize him as superfluous."

"Ouch," said Carl. "That's what I get for letting everyone else do the talking."

To my understanding, Carl is Mr. Weed's partner, came the Dirax's voice. *And he is far from worthless. From my point of view, he may be the more valuable of the pair.*

I was ready to stand up for Carl myself, but I would've done so in a way that painted me in a less derogatory light. "I'm sorry, have we met?" I would've asked his name, but I was fairly sure those were a convention his species didn't subscribe to.

No, said the Dirax, *but I am familiar with your work.*

I elbowed Carl in the ribs. "Look at that. I'm a hot topic around the old InterSTELLA coffee dispenser."

Your error is understandable, said the Dirax, *but you are nonetheless mistaken. I am in GenBorn's employ. I came to investigate the body.* He gestured at the cryo tube.

"Well, that explains how InterSTELLA learned about my last case. So are you some sort of physician? Or mortician?"

Neither, said the Dirax. *My expertise is in Brain function, operation, and maintenance.*

"He did not so much come for body," said Ducic, "as he did for said body's Brain implant."

And all the data within it, said the Dirax.

Tarja stepped forward and rubbed her sleeve against the front of the cryo tube, partially removing some of the frost from the Pseudaglas. "So you removed his Brain?"

Do not be morbid, said the Dirax with a flicker of its antennae. *I am no expert of human anatomy. Besides, that is an unnecessary action. The Brain can be accessed remotely as long as it is powered.*

"Powered?" I said.

"An electrical charge can be passed through frozen tissue, activating Brain function," said Ducic. "We tried this prior to the arrival of GenBorn's employee but to no avail. It would appear we are not as adept at said procedure as we believed."

Do not blame yourself, said the Dirax. *I have determined your efforts failed not due to any technical ineptitude but rather due to hardware incompatibility.*

"Meaning?" asked Tarja.

The Brain implant is non-proprietary.

"Hold on," said Carl. "Are you saying he has a non-GenBorn Brain? I thought your company owned the rights to all sub-cranial digital consciousness implants."

Now you understand our interest in the matter, said the Dirax.

I joined Tarja by the cryo pod. "Mind if I take a look?"

She stepped back and yielded the floor. "Knock yourself out."

I took a peek through the frosted glass. Inside the pod, I spotted a man, slightly taller than me and with less muscle tone, with chin-length brown hair and a prominent brow. His eyelids had been closed, so I couldn't see if he had any ocular implants, but in general he appeared unmodified. In fact, the only interesting thing about him was his attire.

He wore a voluminous long-sleeved shirt that stretched down toward his knees, and over it a tightly-fitting three-buttoned vest of a brilliant magenta. A length of cloth of the same color had been wrapped around the top of his head and tied off in the front, a cross between a bandana and a scarf. Though I couldn't be sure given my angle of observation and the frost, he appeared to be wearing matching fingerless gloves.

"So our suspicions turned out to be well founded," said Ducic.

Correct, said the Dirax. *And the oddities continue beyond Brain composition. I ran a test on the man's blood and found traces of non-proprietary anti-aging antibodies in his system. I've seen similar traces before—it is far more common than theft of our Brain technology—but the particular antibodies I found didn't match those we've come across before.*

"So not only are these folks involved in seemingly impossible raids," said Tarja, "but they've got illicit tech, too? What are the chances of that?"

"If you don't mean the question rhetorically, then I would assume it's similar to the chance of them having only one," said Carl. "The probability of them possessing the sort of tech necessary to attack ships in the manner Ducic has described is supremely unlikely as it is. This doesn't shift the overall probability much."

I turned from the glass and stuck my nose in the conversation before Tarja could showcase her snarling skills. "What about other tests? Have you run this guy through any facial recognition or DNA databases?"

Ducic's nostrils flared. "How incompetent do you assume us to be? That was our first course of action. As you can imagine, we were unsuccessful on both counts. His face did not appear in records, nor did his ancestral markers, though they did indicate he is of mixed European Earth descent."

Tarja snorted. "I could've told you the same by looking at him."

"Am I correct in assuming since he's rocking non-GenBorn hardware, you can't access the data in his Brain?" I asked.

The Dirax's antennae flickered. *That is correct. For now, at least.*

"So, basically," I said, "despite the fact that we've got a deceased captive pirate, we don't know anything about him or his buddies—other than his penchant for odd outer garments."

Yet, emphasized the Dirax.

"Do we have anything else to go on?" I asked.

Ducic nodded. "Once again, follow me."

7

The evidence locker hissed and puffed open upon confirmation of Ducic's thumbprint—or whatever passed for it. His rudimentary hands didn't have thumbs, although I supposed they must've featured some form of print.

Tarja reached a hand in before I had the chance. When she drew it out, she held a sleek pulse pistol.

She pulled back to examine it. "This was on the dead pirate?"

"Correct," said Ducic. "Everything in the locker was."

Tarja turned the weapon over in her hands, examining the components. "It's a beautiful piece. Lightweight composite frame, but with good balance. Not too heavy, not too light. Grip pressure-activated laser sights with optional holoscope. Biometric enabled trigger, if I'm not mistaken. Energy, mass, and combo firing modes, with an extended clip. What sort of wattage is this? I don't see any markings. I'd guess somewhere in the one to two kilowatt range."

"Is that a lot?" I asked.

Tarja gave me one of those dismissive sneers I'd started to grow so fond of. "You don't handle weaponry very often do you?"

"I don't really need to answer that, do I?"

"Wattage doesn't matter so much as other factors," said Tarja. "Voltage, current, and duration of applied current are what really make your targets twitch. But when push comes to shove, more is always better." She smiled, which was the first time I'd seen her do that. Apparently she got off on guns.

She turned the pistol over and inspected a latch to the side of the trigger. "I'm guessing this is the safety? Looks like the gun's set to stun for human targets, though I'm not familiar with this particular signage. Any chance you tried this thing out?"

Ducic nodded. "Said weapon is, indeed, set to stun. You seem to be an enthusiast of pain-causing devices. Are you perchance familiar with the assemblage of this weapon?"

"You mean do I know who made it?" She shook her head. "Doesn't look like it was crafted by any of the major manufacturers. It's a totally different design than I'm used to. Which isn't a bad thing. I like it. A lot. But I'd wager it's a home printed model."

"We suspected as much," said Ducic. "As with the pirate himself, we ran his weaponry though a database search, but results did not strike us."

Carl hummed as he poked his head into the evidence locker.

"Find something interesting, droid?" asked Tarja.

Carl was too predisposed to congeniality to show any displeasure at her tone. "Yes, but my reaction was due to Ducic's news. It doesn't strike me as odd that a band of brigands would print their own weaponry. That would make them harder to track in the event of capture. But I do wonder why they'd bother to create an entirely new design. Why not use one of the many available pulse pistol designs found in the servenets?"

"Maybe they've got a sense of style," I offered. "The dead guy's clothes insinuate as much."

I joined Carl at his side and began extracting the remaining items from the locker. First I found another pistol, same make as the first. Based on Tarja's supposition about the safety, this one had also been set to stun.

"Have the pirates killed anyone during the raids?" I asked.

"Negative," responded Ducic. "If appearances do not deceive, they are a non-violent bunch. Well...that statement is not entirely grounded in fact. Their use of pistols is evidence of the opposite, as is their continued assault on our freighters. But to date they have not ended the life of any of our crew, even following the loss of their own after breach of cargo bay aboard the *Agapetes*. That did not preclude their anger, however. They formed clubs with their hands and used those to discipline the crew. You will see when you watch holovids."

I set the pistol aside and drew another bandana scarf hybrid from the locker. This one was dyed a fierce green color.

"Another headpiece?" I asked.

"Taken from a separate pirate," said Ducic. "He dropped it during proverbial cargo hatch incident. His body was lost, but this portion of his attire was not."

I drew it between my hands. The fabric felt lightweight and breathable, like Linesse but perhaps stretchier. The garment didn't have a tag on it, so I could only assume it, too, was homemade, probably by a bot. I couldn't imagine the pirates practiced needlework in their spare time.

"Seen anything like this before, Carl?"

My partner took the item of clothing. "I can't say I have. In fact, I wouldn't even know what to call it."

Paige? I thought.

Sorry, pal, she chimed in. *Beats me.*

I pictured the pirate, still fresh in my mind's eye, his attire so garish and odd—unlike anything I'd seen around Cetie or in communications or holovids. But his clothing didn't have a historical analogue either, unless it was meant to invoke the image of a water-based pirate from antiquity. Those had worn head wraps of various types, hadn't they?

Tarja muscled in next to me. "Enough with the hijab or burka or do-rag or whatever that is. What else is in the locker?"

Together we extracted and inspected the remaining items, which were few in number. A pair of multitools for unscrewing panels, prying open doors, or defacing walls. A single use compressed acetylene flare which could theoretically be used to cut through a metal bulkhead, assuming you could do so in thirty seconds without melting your hand down to the bone. And an emergency respirator mask with attached miniature oxygen bottle, one I'd hazard had about thirty minutes of breathable air in it. Not that the thing would do much good without a pressure suit in the event of an uncontrolled decompression, which it hadn't, based on the pirate's method of death.

Tarja peered at the interior of the respirator, turning it in the ship's light to get the best angle. "At least this thing has a manufacturer's label. It says...Cluster Consolidated Manufacturing, LLC. There's a serial number, too. Have you looked into that?"

"Affirmative, but with a negative result," said Ducic. "We were unable to locate any manufacturing company by said name."

"Of course not." I shook my head.

Tarja eyed me. "What's that supposed to mean?"

"It means the pirates knew what they were doing," I said. "Not an item recovered from this oddly-dressed space popsicle gives us any traceable clue. Think that's by accident? They made sure not to use stock guns or wear stock clothing. This respirator manufacturer, if it even exists, is probably a front."

Ducic's ears flattened, and his eyes widened, a gesture Paige assured me meant he was crestfallen. "Do you imply what I believe you to? That you have no guess as to how to proceed with this investigation? Perhaps my faith in your intellect was exaggerated."

Tarja snickered. "I think that's safe to say."

"I meant 'your' in the plural sense," said Ducic. "This is grammatically correct, no?"

Tarja's smile vanished.

"I didn't admit to anything of the sort," I said as I returned the multitools and pistol to the locker. "You mentioned holovids. You have surveillance of the pirate attacks?"

"Copious amounts," said Ducic, his ears returning to their regular, forward-facing position. "Of all five attacks, from multiple points of view and covering separate portions of each ship. Enough to occupy one's senses for quite a length."

"Good," I said. "That'll give us something to keep us busy on our way to the *Agapetes*."

Tarja leveled me with a raised eyebrow. She didn't do it as well as Carl did. "You want to visit the *Agapetes*?"

"If it's still close by, yes," I said. "I assume it arrived at the Tau Ceti system if the body recovered aboard was transferred to this ship. It'll be insightful to talk to the crew."

"I do not comprehend," said Ducic. "Did you not hear my mention of the holovids? Are your ear ways blocked by naturally produced waxes and oils?"

"Yes, I got that, thank you," I said. "But in addition to viewing those, we need to talk to the crew. Ask them questions and gauge their responses directly. They might have knowledge the holovids don't, and conducting those conversations remotely, after accounting for transmission lag, isn't as effective. I'd much rather go to them, assuming they're still nearby."

"To my knowledge, freighter *Agapetes* is currently stationed on Varuna in the asteroid belt having its hold repaired and recertified," said Ducic. "Also to be refilled with goods for transport."

"Perfect. That's not so far away, not in celestial terms." I waved at Ducic. "I assume you can get us there?

Vijay said they gave you clearance to access whatever we needed."

Ducic responded with that ears flattened, eyes widened look again. "Data, yes. Physical commodities, no. I may have to requisition a shuttle. To be honest, I am no pilot. Despite the abilities of my Brain, I would not be comfortable in such a scenario."

"You wouldn't," I said. "But Tarja would."

"Not on an InterSTELLA transport," she said. "My own ship, yes."

I gave Tarja my warmest smile. "How nice of you to offer. Let's go then."

The bounty hunter frowned. "Hold on. I didn't—"

"Come on," I said. "We're a team now. I know I spun like a top in zero gravity, but I'm actually pretty handy when I've got two feet under me. And despite your front, I think you're starting to realize I'm not quite as dopey and useless as you first feared. Heck, stick around a year or two and you might even start to like me."

"Doubtful," said Tarja.

"Regardless," I said. "We need a ship and a pilot. You're the latter and have the former. Unless I'm mistaken, as much as you're willing to sit back and accumulate low daily payments, you'd much rather collect on a huge bounty. InterSTELLA's paying our fees, which covers your fuel costs. So...what do you have to lose?"

8

I leaned back in my seat as the holovid cut out, crossing my legs and resting the back of my head against my clasped hands. I chewed on my lip.

We sat in the main cabin of Tarja's ship, a sleek, well-equipped intrastellar cutter by the name of the *Samus Aran,* who apparently was a legendary bounty hunter in her own right. She was a modern ship, and by all measures quite spacious for a scouting vessel, with quarters for three, a cockpit, a galley, and the common room I sat in. Though much of the ship featured stock polished aluminum and molded plastic finishes, Tarja had refurbished broad swaths of it in metallic purple and white. It wasn't the color palate I would've associated with a hardened bounty hunter, but at least it matched her jumpsuit and hair.

The ship wasn't large or powerful enough to have pseudogravity technology aboard, but thanks to our constant linear acceleration, we didn't need it. Tarja hadn't lied about her penchant for pushing the pace, either. I was fairly sure we were pulling about two g's. I felt right at home. Good thing the benches were padded.

Carl rested next to me on the plush built-in wrap-around bench. "Want to start over from the top?"

I mulled Carl's offer. We'd been sitting for hours going through the holovids from the pirate attacks. The raids had ranged from forty-five minutes to an hour in length and each had been recorded thoroughly. I'd been able to insert myself into the action, watch the pirates board the vessels, move through the cabins and subdue the crew, then switch over to the teams emptying the cargo holds, all while sampling vids from the other areas of the ship to make sure nothing escaped my notice. It was exhausting work, even accounting for Paige's helpful curation services.

You think watching *the holovids is exhausting?* asked Paige. *Try* doing *the curation.*

I shook my head. "No point in revisiting the entire collection, Carl. Although I do want to watch the most recent attack again."

"What part?" he asked.

"The one where Captain Horatio is in the command room after the pirates have restrained the crew. I flagged it."

"Anything in particular you're looking for?" asked Carl. "I can keep an eye out—metaphorically speaking, of course."

"I'm not sure," I said. "I just can't get a bead on the pirate captain. The moment when he finds out about his lost crew is the only point in the vids where I see him lose his cool. I thought perhaps there's something to be gleaned from it."

"Fair enough," said Carl.

Got it right here, if you're ready, said Paige.

I gave her the go ahead. My vision of the *Samus Aran* faded and was replaced by the *Agapetes'* command center, a cylindrical room in the middle of the ship that gave the appearance of a turret thanks to the wraparound display wall broadcasting an image from the ship's exterior. The doors into and out of the space were the only things that broke the illusion. A half-dozen captain's chairs faced the outer rim, each of them with various technical displays pasted over the static image of space.

I stood near one of the chairs, superimposed into the holovid via Paige's efforts. Carl hovered to my right, watching everything with me. In front of us in the center of the room, a portion of the ship's crew had been restrained, sitting back to back with their hands zipped tight behind them. Among them were the ship's captain, a slender redhead by the name of Prydwen Rhees, and her first mate Uche Jones, a muscular black man of Tarja's height. Also present were a bruiser with a wide jaw and a flattop and a woman with a fresh face and a pixie cut. I hadn't managed to catch either of the latter two's names.

Pacing in front of the quartet was a man I'd heard other pirates refer to as Captain Horatio. Although the crew around him fluctuated from attack to attack, he'd led the assault on each of the five targeted InterSTELLA ships.

I paused the holovid and stepped toward the captain. Like the frosty specimen locked within the *Snowbell's* medical bay, he sported an odd assortment of clothing.

His shirt was shorter and less voluminous than the mystery pirate's, with square French cuffs and prominent pleats. A puffy bright yellow ascot poured from his unbuttoned collar, and instead of a vest, the man wore a suit jacket with short sleeves—not cut off, either. They were intentionally short, as evidenced by the stitching. Atop his head, I found another of the bandana-ish sorts of garments, this one in the same bright yellow as his ascot. While fashion varied among the brigands, they all wore some iteration of the brightly dyed headgear, and always in a single solid color.

The captain's hair poured out the back of his headpiece in a long ponytail. I peered at the yellow cloth. Were the sides of his head shaved? The rag should've been puffier at the sides if not.

"Is everything okay?" asked Carl.

"Just getting a closer look." I stepped back. "Let's keep going, Paige."

Captain Horatio continued to pace. He shook his head and sneered. "I's must hand it to ye's, Capin Rhees. Ye's put up a good fight. Better 'an 'ose other skraggin' capins and their skraggin' crews. Lightweights and poseurs, all 'em. Ne'er mind their lack of preparedness, or that when they's so lucky as to lay hands on a weapon 'o some sort, they could'na hit the broad side o' a freighter from within 'tis own hold. Ney, they's lacked ingenuity. But ye's? Ye's got that. Ye's skraggin' got it, all right."

Rhees stared him down with ice in her eyes. "What did you expect? That we'd roll over and die?"

"Die?" Horatio's eyes widened. "Ney, please don't. That'd cause untold difficulties. Suffer through waves o' internal turmoil? 'Tis fine. Even external suffering. 'Tis fine. But let's all keep our heads, ney?"

Rhees ground her teeth. She was small, but spunky.

"Don'na gimme that look," said Horatio. "I didn'a even like the skraggers ye's spaced. Fortunata and De-Navarre. Sloppy, they's was. Sloppiness gets ye's killed."

The man with the wide jaw and the flattop spoke. "So how the hell are *you* alive? You're sloppy as shit."

Horatio took that as an affront, either to his manner or his fashion. He planted a boot in the man's face, sending the poor woman zip tied at his back tumbling to the floor as well. Flattop grunted. To her credit, Pixie didn't even squeal.

Horatio snapped at his subordinates, two of which stood against the wall with pulse pistols in hand. "Where's that skraggin' engineer? I thought ye's said he's on his way."

He kept using that word, *skragging*. I'd figured out it was an insult, but had he made it up? I'd never heard it before. Perhaps it was popular in pirate communities.

The pirate stammered. "I...Uh..."

Fate saved him. Another pirate entered with a handsome gentleman in tow, one with styled hair and a tightly trimmed auburn beard.

"'Tis 'im?" asked Horatio.

The new pirate nodded. "He's the one who locked down the corridor outside the cargo bay and o'errode the safeties. Matched the logs to 'is Brain."

Horatio approached the man, who stood about a half a head taller than him. "What's ye'ss name?"

"Watkins." His face said he wasn't inclined to elaborate. Of course, I'd already watched the vid, so I knew he wouldn't.

Horatio nodded as he absorbed the information. "Watkins. 'Ats a good name. I likes it. And I like ye's. Gutsy. Decisive. Creative. Kinda person I like in my crews."

Horatio slammed a fist into Watkins' stomach without warning. A pained groan left the man's lips as he doubled over. Horatio slammed him to the floor with another pair of punches to the head, then went to work on his midsection with his boot. Rhees bellowed for him to stop, and whether by her appeal or his own choice, he did. All told he only hit the man a half-dozen times.

Horatio ignored Rhees and the uncertain looks of the rest of the *Agapetes'* crew. "'Jes 'cause I like ye's, Watkins, don'a mean I can let ye'ss defiance go unpunished. 'Jes be glad I'm the merciful sort."

He slammed one last boot into the man's groin, causing a sharp gasp of pain.

One of the pirates eyed his captain with uncertainty. "Uh, Capin...I thought them's jewels was off limits?"

"One kick won' hurt," said Horatio. "E'll be fine. Now get this skraggin' sack of scat outta my sight afore I do somethin' I and all the rest o' us might regret. I'm gonna check on the transport."

I paused the holovid again. I walked over to the captain and studied his visage. What was his game? He seemed like a violent man but oddly restrained. Did he fear capture and the resulting punishment he might receive if he were? Was that why he avoided killing anyone, even the man responsible for the death of three of his own men? And where was that accent from? I couldn't place it, but the universe was a big place.

I pursed my lips. The quality of the holovid security footage was top notch, but could it really reveal to me the measure of the man? The subtleties in his eyes?

"Rich," said Carl.

"Yes?"

"Ducic's here."

"Thanks."

The holovid faded, replaced with the purple and white of the *Samus Aran's* interior. Ducic ambled over from the direction of his quarters. I wanted to say he looked annoyed, but again, I knew nothing of Tak facial expression and body language.

"Making yourself comfortable?" I asked.

He tilted his head as he approached me. "First you question my translucency, now this. I assure you, my form is quite rigid. Are you under illusions regarding my physiology? If so, there are texts I can refer you to."

"I simply wondered how you were adapting to your quarters," I said. "I know they're meant for a human."

"Oh," said Ducic. "In that case, your concern is appreciated but unwarranted. My species is used to lazing in confined spaces, and we do not lay prone on our spinal cords as you do. During bouts of rest, we simply fold our legs underneath us and relax our crest muscles. Although, to be most honest, a good mat upon which to rest my barrel would not be unwelcome."

Paige flashed an image of a horse in the corner of my vision, one with an arrow pointing to its belly and the word 'Barrel' underneath it. I gave her my silent thanks.

"So, Ducic," I said. "I've got a question for you."

"By all means, expel it over me."

"I've gone through the holovids from the various attacks and I was wondering about external surveillance."

"What of it?" asked Ducic.

"Do you have any?" I asked. "I'd like to know what the pirates' ship looked like. Even if it doesn't have a visible serial number on its hull, we might be able to track it by its manufacture."

"Apologies, Rich," said Ducic. "But the ships' external holovids would not help you in this regard."

"Why not?" I asked.

"You recall our discussion of the warp bubble?" he said. "It is a severe compression of space time. Light cannot escape it, and therefore external cameras are not able to see past edge of bubble."

I glanced at Carl to see if he followed. "I thought you said the pirates warped into the freighters' bubbles."

Ducic's muzzle wrinkled. "I think I understand your confusion. You overestimate size of the warp bubble. Its creation is exceptionally energy intensive, and said energy requirement is size dependent. Therefore bubble is created as small as feasible. It is akin to a film over the surface of ship."

"So how did the pirates get into—or onto—the bubble?" I asked. "How did they get on the ships?"

"It is uncertain," said Ducic. "Possibly their bubble melded with those of attacked freighters at the interlocks. That, at least, would explain said lack of visual display from external cameras. It would create a highly energy inefficient configuration, but less so than expanding bubble to encompass both ships."

"How would such a task be achieved?" asked Carl.

Ducic's ears flattened. "I have no idea."

"You're a physicist, aren't you?" I said. "Surely you must have some guess."

"Hypersurfaces are not my area of expertise."

"So what is?" I asked.

"Relativistic quantum field theory," he said. "Pseudogravitation, specifically."

I blinked. I hadn't expected that answer. I stored it for future reference. "So, going back to my original question, we don't have any idea what sort of ship the pirates captained?"

"Negative," said Ducic.

"What about the crew of the attacked freighters?" I said. "I don't suppose any of them boarded the pirate ship at any point in time?"

"To best of my knowledge, no," said Ducic. "If so, it should be obvious from holovids. Can I ask what prompts this query?"

As good as the holovids were, they contained a few gaps. For one, there weren't holorecorders in the ships' airlocks, merely right outside them in the adjoining hallways. Similarly, the holorecorders in the cargo bay were all pointed at the cargo itself. When I'd inserted myself into the vids to look around, the cargo doors themselves had remained grayed out. I could see the pirates and their transport droids shuffling in and out, but the recording lost them at the doors.

"Don't worry about it," I said. "I'm just trying to gather all the evidence I can. Expand my knowledge base."

Ducic's ears perked. "If that is your goal, I can assist. I enjoy spirited debates over physical nature and principles, and I find the solitude of my assigned quarters has become wearisome."

"I, ah...would love to," I said as I stood. "But I've got to take a rain check. I've been meaning to talk to Tarja. Carl, on the other hand, would love to chat."

"What?" said Carl. "I—"

Take one for the team, buddy, I sent him via Brain. *You'll get more out of it than I would.*

He didn't even fight back with a snarky reply. What a guy.

9

I found Tarja in the ship's cockpit, her legs propped up on the dash and her eyes trained on the vast expanse of stars outside the Pseudaglas windows. She did a double take when she spotted me. Subtle, but I noticed it.

"Surprised to see me?" I asked.

"You finish the holovids?" she asked.

I nodded. "You?"

"Of course I did."

I sighed. "It's not a race. I feel rather silly reminding you, mostly because Carl, Ducic, and I are all aboard your ship, but we're a team now. We'll be more effective if we work together."

Tarja rolled her eyes. "Yeah, well I work better alone."

"Have you ever tried otherwise?"

Tarja leveled me with a withering glance. Clearly there was more to the narrative than I'd suspected.

My bounty hunter host occupied the cockpit's only chair, so I leaned against the console, hoping I wouldn't activate anything with my meaty bottom. I was curious about the source of her glare, but I was smart enough not to ask.

"So..." I said. "You catch many thieves? Or brigands or escapees or whoever else people pay you to go after?"

Tarja looked down her sharp, slender nose at me. "You've seen my ship, right?"

"That doesn't mean anything," I said. "I'm independently wealthy. For all I know, you're also a legacy marijuana farmer's grandchild with too much cash on her hands and without a sense of purpose in her life."

"You lack a sense of purpose?"

"We were talking about you."

Tarja sighed. "What do you want?"

"I'm extending an olive branch, which is a metaphor I definitely won't be using on Ducic. Basically, I'm trying to get to know you."

"Oh, that's so sweet," said Tarja, clasping her hands and widening her eyes. "You want to be *buddies*? Let me ping all my girlfriends to share the good news. They'll be positively ecstatic."

"You really *do* work alone all the time, don't you?" I said.

She dropped the act. "What's that supposed to mean?"

"Look, I work in a partnership, just me and Carl, but even I know when you assemble a team as, let's say, *diverse* as this one, it's beneficial to understand each other's strengths and weaknesses. What if we get in a jam? We'll need to know who takes point and who brings up the rear. Who do we defer to on technical matters? Who's in charge? That sort of thing."

Tarja shifted her feet to the floor and leaned forward. "Let's be clear then. *I'm* in charge. And as far as my strengths, I excel at two things: kicking ass and taking names."

"What about your weaknesses?"

"What weaknesses?"

I tried not to roll my eyes. I mostly succeeded. "As reassuring as your braggadocio is, it's not particularly telling."

"You think I'm lying about my accomplishments?" said Tarja. "I'm telling you, I *earned* this ship. I didn't inherit it from some doped up grandfather without any worthwhile heirs to pass his fortune to. And if you have a problem with my success I can introduce to my top of the line airlock system. Pro tip: I know how to bypass the fail safes."

By this point I knew it was all an act, but I still had to force myself to say calm. Letting myself be goaded would only egg her on. "As I said, I'm trying to get to know you. That includes learning about your accomplishments."

"So you want me to regale you with stories of my perilous adventures and cunning victories?" she said. "Like my defeat of the pirate Tellerman Bundy during our dogfight in the tail of Marshall's Comet? Or the time I captured the Tryzeki broodmates outside the Pleasuredome orbiting Gleise five eighty-one c? Or how I tricked Paul 'The Cross' Richardson and Korvik Durulaque into letting me onto their ship, whereupon I hacked their mainframe and spaced the pair?"

"Well...yes," I said.

"Hah." Tarja rolled her eyes again. "You would."

"What is it about taunting others you take such pleasure in?"

"It's not everybody," said Tarja. "Just you. And maybe your droid partner. And possibly Ducic, depending on my mood. Let's say none of the personalities in this batch I was assigned are my type."

"You have a type?"

She gave me another of those cold glares. "Are you ever going to leave me alone?"

"Depends," I said. "Are you ever going to tell me one of those stories?"

"Fine. Which one?"

"I love a good ruse," I said. "Tell me how you tricked Paul 'The Cross' Whatshisname and that other doofus into letting you onto their ship."

Tarja shifted her eyes to the windows. "In retrospect, maybe that's not the best one. Why don't I tell you about the Pleasuredome?"

As enticing as hearing about a place called the Pleasuredome was, my curiosity had been piqued. "What's wrong with the other story?"

"I don't know," said Tarja. "Look, I hadn't planned on mentioning that one. It just...popped to mind. It doesn't paint me in a good light."

"Because you spaced the dudes?"

Tarja's head turned, and she drilled me with an icy gaze that made her previous attempts seem toasty. "I don't regret that. Those bastards got what they deserved." She dropped her eyes and looked away. "Besides, the bounty on the pair said dead or alive. I got my SEUs all the same."

I scratched my chin. "So—"

"Look, I don't want to be a dick," said Tarja, which I knew was a lie. "But we're almost at the halfway point of this trip, and I need to prepare for the turn. Why don't you sod off for a while and bug someone else? Grab a snack or take a nap or something. I don't really care what so long as you get your ass off my control panel."

I stood, liberating my rear from the ship's delicate instruments. "Yeah, sure. I'll warn Ducic. I don't think he cares much for zero grav."

I headed down the hatch to the main cabin, wondering to myself what the real story behind Tarja and the two spaced pirates was.

10

I awoke to a thump, notably that of my head making contact with the bulkhead above my cot. I blinked and tried to turn over, only to find myself spinning in place near the ceiling. Apparently, the *Samus Aran* had finished her deceleration while I'd slept, as evidenced by my weightlessness.

Carl thought about engaging the bed's straps while you slept, said Paige. *Ultimately he didn't, as you can clearly tell.*

I felt my forehead. No bump, no blood. Probably wouldn't even leave a mark. "And why didn't he?"

He thought it would teach you a lesson. Guess he was wrong. He's in the main cabin if you need him. We should be docking with the Agapetes soon.

I shoved myself off the ceiling and used a sideways push when I reached the floor to get me to the windows. I latched onto a handhold and steadied myself without banging a single one of my body parts against the wall. Amazingly enough, my stomach felt fine, and I didn't feel the least bit disoriented.

"You know, I think I'm starting to get the hang of this," I told Paige.

Well, of course, she said. *You've experienced a whopping thirty-five minutes of microgravity over the past sixteen hours. You're a regular space marine.*

I pressed my nose to the window and gazed into the landscape outside. Thousands of points of light glittered as far as the eye could see, as if I were looking at the densest portion of the Milky Way, but I knew they weren't stars. They flickered haphazardly, some of them winking out of existence, either from their irregular albedo or due to occlusion effects, as others sprang to life under the steady illumination of Tau Ceti.

We'd arrived in the asteroid field, and below us, increasing in size as we approached, was Varuna, the second largest body in the belt. With a radius of a few hundred kilometers, it dominated the lower half of my field of vision, but only because we were so close. On a celestial scale, it was a gnat's fart. It barely pulled a fortieth of a g, which was why I'd impacted the ceiling. Compared to the ship's deceleration, Varuna's tug was like that of an anemic baby.

Below us, I spotted what at first appeared to be an enormous crater, at least twenty kilometers in diameter, but as we drew nearer, it became obvious the gaping hole was man made. A strip mine.

A wide path rotated around the interior of the hole, delving ever deeper as it circled toward the center. Metallic flashes gleamed here and there, massive cranes and transport crawlers and freighters, many of them in motion, as well as the static bundle of structures to the right of the excavation site—housing for the colony of a hundred or so that lived on the asteroid at the base of the mine. It didn't seem like many given the sheer size of the dig, but the vast majority of the work was performed by bots and droids of various sizes, shapes, and forms. The human and alien contingents were primarily in place for engineering, maintenance, and security purposes.

The door to my chamber puffed and I heard Carl's voice. "Ah. You're up." He floated over next to me.

"It's beautiful, in a sense," I said.

Carl shrugged. "I know my aesthetic sensibilities don't match your own, but even accounting for that, I'm struggling to see what's appealing about a strip mine."

"I couldn't say, exactly," I said. "Maybe the knowledge of what it took to pull off makes it more impressive. The sheer size is overwhelming."

"It's always about size with you humans, isn't it?"

I gave my partner a look. "Was that a genitalia joke?"

"Well, joke might be stretching it, judging by your reaction." He nodded toward the window. We'd been travelling at a constant speed, but the closer we got, the faster we appeared to be moving. Our target, a hefty cargo ship which I assumed was the *Agapetes,* grew larger and larger. "Looks like we're almost there. Join me in the main cabin?"

I nodded. We both propelled ourselves out the door and into the common room where we found Ducic with his legs tucked tightly underneath him and his head shrunk back into his neck as far as it would go. He floated slowly to one side, rotating slightly as he did so. He wrinkled his muzzle and flattened his ears against his head fiercely.

"You doing okay?" I asked.

"If by that you intend to determine my state of being, then no," he said.

"Are you going to puke?" I wondered how bad that would be. Taks ate mostly roughage, didn't they?

"I am in no danger of expelling partially digested foodstuffs," he said. "As I have explained already, our bodies do not behave similarly. My balance centers are, however, extremely sensitive to motion incurred under the lack of a gravitational pull. This is, I think, similar to your species' sensation of vertigo."

"That bad, huh?"

"I am contemplating death as a preferable alternative. Could your droid help still my rotation, perchance?"

Carl sprang into action. Though his base programming only dictated he be compassionate and subservient to humans, he was a good guy at heart. Besides, Ducic asked nicely.

The ship jolted again, and a loud clanking sound reverberated through the hull. Tarja dropped through the cockpit hatch, rebounded off the floor, and flew off in the direction of the airlock. "We've docked, gents. Pseudograv should be kicking in as soon as the *Agapetes'* power connects."

Ducic made some subtle motions with his hands that I interpreted as a prayer. I headed after Tarja while Carl deftly navigated Ducic after us as if he were driving a hoverlift.

The pseudogravity hummed to life while the airlock cycled. Ducic's face lit up like a casino holodisplay, and I instructed Paige to save the image for future reference in case I ever forgot what Tak happiness looked like.

The door opened, and on the other side stood a man in a sharply-pressed two piece navy blue InterSTELLA uniform. His jaw stuck out, giving him a rather fierce look, and his straight-standing hair had been checked with calipers to make sure it was of a uniform length. A pulse pistol jutted from a holster strapped to his side, but I couldn't tell whether it was set to stun or kill. I recognized him instantly from the security holovids.

His voice rolled slightly when he spoke, not from a speech impediment but from an accent I couldn't place. "Tarja Olli? Rich Weed? And Ducic?" Taks didn't have last names. "I am chief warrant officer Valente Urrupain. Captain Rhees is expecting you. Come with me."

He turned and headed off down the corridor, and we all followed. Given the size of the freighter, I'd expected to have time to size Urrupain up and perhaps even get to know him before we rendezvoused with the captain, but barely had we turned a couple corners before we piled into a small lift and shot up to the command center level. Thanks to Ducic's bulk, Tarja, Valente, Carl, and I got real cozy during the fifteen second trip. I might've even made it to second base—with Carl, unfortunately.

When the door opened, we all spilled out and flexed our ribs in the newfound space before waltzing up a ramp into the command center.

The display walls currently showed a panoramic view of Varuna's surface, complete with the yawning edge of the strip mine and the gleaming, boxy colony not far from there. Captain Rhees, dressed in a baggy yellow commander's uniform that clashed horribly with her copper-colored hair, stood in front of the display, cycling through readings via Brain. Her first mate, Uche Jones, stood at her side, tall and sleek and without a single follicle on the top of his head. He wore a navy blue uniform similar to our escort's. His fit him better than the captain's did, but only slightly. The seams at his shoulders threatened to burst, and I reminded myself to stay on his good side. Even with my kickboxing background, I wouldn't want to take him.

Urrupain cleared his throat. "Captain? I've brought the investigators."

I'm sure the captain heard our approach, but she waited for Valente's address before turning. Her cheeks were smoother than I remembered from the holovids and not flushed from anger, but her eyes seemed cool and unflinching. In that respect, she reminded me of Tarja. Perhaps an icy streak was a prerequisite for becoming the captain of one's own vessel—although in Tarja's case, she'd established her position by default.

Rhees surveyed us thoroughly as Uche joined her at her side. Based on the disgruntled look on her face, I'd wager she didn't care for what she saw.

"Alright, listen up," she said. "I'm Captain Prydwen Rhees and the *Agapetes* is my ship. There are a few things you should know about me. I don't tolerate inefficiency among my crew, I highly dislike red tape and obstructionist bullshit, and I hate—and I do mean HATE—being late. The *Agapetes* is current parked on Varuna for two reasons and two reasons only. To have its external cargo bay doors and adjoining hatches checked for faults, repaired where necessary, and safety tested, and to load its hull for a return trip to Mars. We WILL be leaving at InterSTELLA's prescribed departure time for our vessel, which is in roughly fifty standard galactic hours.

"You may have noticed that among the two reasons I mentioned we're parked on Varuna, I didn't include babysitting a bunch of wannabe detectives and mercenaries and researchers, or playing tour guide, or answering a bunch of stupid questions from anyone who thinks they understand intergalactic safety better than those of us who live it on a daily basis. Understood?"

I nodded. Tarja took a more courageous approach. "Look, Captain, we—"

"I'm not finished," said Rhees with a snap of her teeth. "Now, while keeping in mind everything I've already made clear to you, I'll also add I've received word from the head of security aboard the *Snowbell* that I'm to comply with your requests to the best of my ability and assist fully in your investigation. You should know my definitions of the words 'best' and 'fully' differ from his. I do, however, follow orders, which is why I'm assigning my first mate, Uche Jones—" She gestured to her side. "—to the task. He's supremely capable, and to put it mildly, grossly overqualified for such an assignment. Any questions?"

I tentatively raised my hand. "Can I ask you about the pirates?"

"No," said Rhees. "Anything else?"

"That's not really what I meant by that question," I said.

Rhees pierced me with her gaze. "I know what you meant. Didn't you watch the damn holovids provided to you? You saw what happened. Honestly, I have no idea why you're here. Everything you need to know has been recorded and documented thoroughly. You should feel lucky I've assigned Jones to you, not only because he's my best, but because he's far more patient than I am. Now...Jones?"

The tall, muscular man waved us forward. "Come on. I'll show you around."

11

"So, anywhere in particular you'd like to start?" asked Uche.

"How about the cargo bay," I said. "I had a few things I wanted to look at. Maybe afterwards we could sit down for a chat."

Uche nodded. As soon as we'd stepped out of earshot of the command center, Tarja turned to him. "So what the hell is her problem?"

Uche offered a small smile as he walked. "Captain Rhees? I know she comes across as severe, but you have to get to know her. She's a fantastic commander, and I feel lucky to serve under her."

"None of which excuses her personality," said Tarja.

I had to choke back a laugh. The thought of Tarja finding fault in Captain Rhees for her brusque, cold demeanor was too much. Did she not see the similarities? They were even both captains, for crying out loud.

"You can't fault her for that," said Uche. "The pirate attack has us all on edge. *Still.* We'd been prepared for the possibility, of course, but none of us had ever experienced anything of the sort. It caught us off guard. I mean, we were attacked and robbed at gunpoint."

"Pulse gunpoint," said Tarja.

"Just because those things were set to stun doesn't mean they couldn't have been switched over to their lethal setting at any moment," said Uche. "You watched the vids, right? You saw that pirate captain, what he did to Watkins. He was totally unstable."

"None of which excuses your captain's behavior," said Tarja.

Uche's smile faded. "Look, I'm trying to be civil, but I won't have you speaking ill of my commanding officer. And you're not thinking about the larger picture. Yes, we were outnumbered three to one, and yes, we were attacked by pirates with tech nobody understands. But that doesn't mean we don't all look like jackasses now. We're one of the victims. And to *those* bunch of pirates, no less. I mean...well, never mind."

"No, I get it," I said. "I noticed it, too. In the vids. The pirates seemed...kind of dumb. I mean, don't get me wrong. They were organized. Efficient. Good shots with those pulse pistols. And the team of loader bots they used to clean out your cargo hold operated with absurd speed. Still, I don't know if it was their accents or the conversations they carried among themselves, but I didn't get any particular vibe of intelligence from them. All except for that Horatio guy. I couldn't get a good read on him except for his explosive anger and unstable nature."

"I know, right?" said Uche. "That's the worst part. How did *they* get their hands on faster than light, warp bubble interaction tech? I mean, seriously? How is that even possible? You. Ducic. I read the bios they sent over from the *Snowbell*. You're a physicist, right? Do you have a clue?"

"It is physically possible," said our resident Tak. "But unfortunately, my knowledge of physics does not help decipher mechanisms for their mid-warp docking. This is, I believe, more of an engineering problem."

Ducic's statement struck a chord with me. If he was right, why hadn't Vijay assigned us an engineer in addition to a physicist?

We rounded a corner, and a high-pitched, mouse-like voice sounded behind us. "Uche? Later, when you're not busy, can we go over some drive logs? There are a few discrepancies I noticed with the net field flux measurements."

I glanced into the corridor and found the fresh-faced woman with the pixie haircut from the holovids. She was slight and not particularly tall but not quite small enough to explain her voice.

"You bet," said Uche over his shoulder. "I'll ping you when I'm done."

We kept walking. Once again, when out of earshot, Tarja asked, "And that was?"

"Persephone Kass," said Uche. "She's in engineering with Watkins."

"How many of you are there total?" I'd only spotted six on the vids, but then again, Paige had curated the content for me to give me the most relevant stuff.

"Eight," said Uche. "The three of us you met in the command room, Kass, Watkins, Fillion, Wong, and Vijitpongpun."

"Vijit-what?" I said.

"Vijitpongpun," said Uche. "That's her last name. We call her that partly out of convention and partly because her first name is Kittiporn. She's of Earthen Thai ancestry and even *she* thinks it's a little inappropriate."

"No droids?" I asked.

"No more than on any other InterSTELLA vessel," said Uche.

I was on the verge of asking why when Paige filled me in. *I think the reason is twofold. First, droids are useless when faced with human on human conflict. Even something as simple as a price negotiation between parties can be complicated, never mind something more dangerous like a pirate attack. Second, InterSTELLA has a history of hiring only humans, and later any organic life. They were founded in the era of massively disruptive overpopulation on the planet Earth, after all.*

You know this off the top of your head? I asked.

The Agapetes' servenets were very welcoming, said Paige. *At least for all the stuff that didn't require a clearance level. I've learned a lot about the history of space travel—as told through the lens of the galaxy's largest intergalactic transportation provider, that is. I'm sure it's completely unbiased.*

I heard the puff of a door, and Uche waved us forward. "Alright, here we go. This is the main corridor adjacent to the cargo bay. You'll need a suit to enter storage. We have the capacity to pressurize the bay, but we don't do it unless there's a need, and for metals like we normally transport, there isn't. Same thing for pseudogravity. Keeping it on in the bay is a huge waste of energy, so we don't. The suits are in the built-ins at the ends, organized by height. Girth adjusts automatically so long as you fit the mean size parameters, which all of you do. The airlock on our right is the one Wilkins overrode to eliminate some of the pirates. We had to perform minor repairs on the door and the Pseudaglas barrier, but it's all set. The only security checks we still have to run are in the bay on the main cargo door, which, again, is unpressurized at the moment."

Jones nodded to Ducic. "We don't have any suits to fit Taks, so you won't be able to join them. I'll show you to our break room. For the rest of you, I'll stay in Brain contact, so if you have any questions, let me know. If you see loader bots coming over from the direction of the mine, please stay out of their way. The microgravity is hard enough to deal with without interference."

Ducic didn't look particularly bent out of shape as Uche led him off. I couldn't imagine he relished the idea of suiting up—not with his physiology and T-rex arms.

I sifted through the drawers in search of something that would fit me while Tarja headed straight for the cubbies with the helmets.

"No suit?" I asked.

"What do you think I'm wearing?"

She removed gloves from her pockets and donned them, clipping them into place at the wrists. Apparently her purple jumpsuit provided some function with its form.

I slipped into my own suit, a metallic silver and dull gray ordeal with the InterSTELLA logo pasted across the front. I waited a moment as it self-adjusted to my meaty, Cetie figure.

Carl stood at the airlock, waiting on us organic types to finish protecting our fluid-filled organs. "Ready?"

Tarja snapped a helmet into place, and I did the same. "Ready."

We went through the airlock, sitting through its noisy cycles and enduring the pseudograv cutoff, before hopping into the massive, open cargo bay.

It was huge, at least fifty meters long and twice as wide, with heavy girders and trusses crisscrossing the ceiling, but what really struck me was the *silence.*

I'd been in spacesuits before, but except for one occasion it was on exoplanets and moons and Meertori cruisers, bodies with atmospheres that were either toxic or too high or low of a pressure for human consumption. Varuna didn't have an atmosphere at all. No air meant no sound. All I could hear was the clump of my feet against the floor and my own steady breathing.

It didn't last. Jones cut in via Brain. *Hey, I'm back.*

I turned to see him in the connecting corridor behind the Pseudaglas. He waved. *Again, let me know you have any questions. Feel free to look around.*

The right half of the bay had already been filled with cargo: stacks of dull metal blocks reaching nearly from floor to ceiling, with only narrow passages in between every ten meters. A flexible net covered each pile and connected at the bottom corners to an enormous metal pallet.

What's that stuff? I asked.

Tungsten, came Uche's voice. *You know. The only thing they refine on Varuna.*

No need to get snarky, I sent back.

I hopped toward the open bay doors, through which I could see the icy, grey expanse of our asteroid host. *What was in your last shipment?* I asked Uche. *The one that got hijacked?*

Iridium.

From?

The Sol belt.

I reached the apex of my hop and descended slowly toward the floor. *What can you tell me about the actual theft of the cargo? Not the pirates who subdued you and your crew. The guys transferring the metals.*

Brain communications didn't transfer sarcasm well, but I inferred it. *Did you watch the holovids?*

Yes, I replied.

Then you know as much as I do, said Uche. *As much as any of us do, really. The rest of the crew and I were too busy trying to hold off the intruders to worry about the cargo. Even Wilkins, who overrode the airlock, did it remotely. But the vids show it clearly. They used coordinated swarms of miniature thruster bots. Given the weight of the metals, they'd be useless even under light gravitational pulls, but during a zero g assault like we experienced, they did the trick.*

And did the pirates take all the cargo?

Pretty much, said Uche. *Why do you ask?*

Just curious, I replied.

I arrived at the exterior bay doors. While the hauntingly beautiful expanse of Varuna beckoned, I made sure not to stray from the ship. I wouldn't do well out there. One wrong step and I might hurtle into the asteroid belt.

Not unless you think you can reach a velocity of four hundred meters per second on a single jump, said Paige.

I was kidding, I replied.

Carl joined me at my side. I knew he was a droid and all, but it still felt odd to have him standing next to me in his street clothes.

Looking for anything in particular? he asked.

Just the overall condition, I said. *I'm trying to gauge if the doors were forced. Any input, Jones?*

Unfortunately, no, he said. *We suspect the pirates hacked into our ship's mainframe and opened them that way.*

I frowned, but upon visual inspection, it did seem as if the doors hadn't been forced. No scratches, dents, or gouges upon the seals—assuming, of course, they hadn't been replaced.

I'll need the ship's access logs, I told Uche.

You think we haven't already looked for intrusions?

I'll still need them, I said.

There was a pause on Uche's end. *I'll see what I can do. No promises. Ducic might be the only one with clearance to see them.*

Tarja cut in. A red light flickered in the corner of my vision, indicating it was a private channel. *Rich. We need to talk.*

Yeah?

What the hell are we doing?

What do you mean? I asked.

You really expect to break this piracy case by examining the nicks on the bay doors?

I'm an investigator, I said. *This is what I do.*

Tarja didn't respond, but I spotted her shaking her head.

I glanced toward the cargo. *Want to check it out, Carl?*

He nodded. *Sure.*

Uche interrupted before I reached the peak of my next hop. *Look, guys, I don't want to tell you how to do your jobs, but could you maybe skip the tungsten maze? If you were hoping to find clues left from our iridium shipment, that's all gone. Plus there's a crawler headed this way with more cargo, and the bots on Varuna aren't the newest models. If they run into you, it could give them fits. I'll give you one guess who Captain Rhees is going to blame for that.*

Yes, said Tarja. *For the love of God, lets head back in.*

Why so eager? I asked. *You're a spacer. You practically live in a suit.*

Tarja crossed her arms. *I'm bored out of my mind, that's why. And we're getting nowhere. Are those good enough reasons for you?*

On the second point I had to disagree, but I kept it to myself for the time being. I nodded and hopped toward the airlock upon meeting the ground.

12

I sat in a chair in the *Agapetes'* break room, nursing a weak cup of coffee. Tarja had excused herself to the *Samus Aran,* and I'd sent Carl after her, mostly to make sure she wouldn't try to take off without me. Ducic stood to my side next to the room's automated beverage dispenser. He'd refused to partake in the coffee, but he'd accepted a mug of reconstituted wheatgrass juice, which sounded positively horrifying.

I took a sip of my *café au lait* and grimaced. Of course, on second thought, maybe Ducic knew something I didn't.

"Is the coffee always this bad?" I asked.

Uche sat across from me in the small room. He'd neglected to take a beverage of any kind. "Honestly, I don't even notice it. They're space rations. Nothing's ever fresh."

I shook my head. "Over a thousand years of space travel and technological advancements, and we still can't make preserved food taste good. Where did we go wrong?"

"I think everyone stopped caring when they figured out how to use Brain technology to activate taste receptors artificially," said Uche.

It was possible. If I really wanted to, I could activate a realistic Brain simulation in which I sipped on the galaxy's finest coffee and nibbled on decadent pastries and chocolates, but I couldn't override the taste sensations produced from actually eating and drinking. GenBorn had locked that portion of the Brain software to users after a high-profile case involving a meal replacement product by the name of Soylent Brown, which was largely composed of wood pulp and maggot protein. Its consumers had been so Brain taste dependent they couldn't tell the difference.

I set my coffee down on the table before me. "So I take it you don't particularly miss the comforts of home."

Uche's eyebrows furrowed. "What do you mean by that?"

"I'm just wondering why you joined InterSTELLA," I said. "Travelling through space, seeing the galaxy, all that jazz. I admit, it sounds tempting, but I have to figure the reality is less glamorous."

Uche snorted and shook his head.

"Sorry," I said. "Did I touch a nerve?"

The muscular first mate sized me up. "You're a Cetiean, aren't you? You'd have to be based on your build."

"That's right."

"Tell me," he said. "What sort of monthly government work stipend do you get?"

Paige had to remind me. "A thousand SEUs."

"Which I assume is plenty to live off, as long as you're not extravagant," he said. "That's why you see so many bots and droids on Cetie. The government can't entice people to come out of their own Brains, much less their apartments. Why would they? The bots do better jobs. Human workers aren't needed. But the economics are different when you have a population several orders of magnitude greater on a planet that's substantially smaller."

"You're from Earth, then?" I asked.

"Yeah. Born in the Confederated States of Central Africa," he said. "Want to take a wild stab at what my government work stipend was back home?"

"A lot less than a thousand SEUs a month, I'd assume."

Uche snapped his fingers and pointed at me. "Bingo. Back at home, my family could barely afford an apartment the size of this room, and I grew up eating hydroponic potato cubes and fishmeal protein steaks. That's the real reason I don't mind the food here. And mine isn't an uncommon tale. Government stipends are low all over Earth, in every nation and confederacy. I'd argue artificially low, specifically so people will move away. That's why I joined InterSTELLA."

I sat there twiddling my thumbs and performing lip gymnastics. I hadn't meant to bring up a sore subject.

Uche cracked a smile. "Although...I have to admit, I did always harbor dreams of travelling the stars. So you weren't totally wrong about that."

"How's it been?" I asked.

He shrugged. "Mostly as you've suspected. I stare at narrow ship corridors a lot, and when they let me out, it's mostly to asteroids."

Ducic slurped his wheatgrass. I'd almost forgotten he was there, which was difficult to do in a small room with a five hundred kilo Tak at your side.

"I must admit," he said, "this story resonates with familiarity for me."

I rested my arm against the back of my bench. "Is your home planet overpopulated, too?"

"Unassailably so," said Ducic. "You see, in commune of my birth, there was—"

Uche leaned forward. "Look, I'm sorry to interrupt, Ducic. You seem like an okay dude, and under other circumstances, I'd, ah...*love* to hear about your upbringing. But as I've tried to point out on numerous occasions, I *do* have other things to do, not least of which is meeting up with Kass. So unless you have other pressing questions...?"

I didn't have anything specific to ask, mostly because I hadn't gotten a grasp on my own line of thought yet, but that didn't mean I was done. Really what I wanted was to isolate the crew one by one, talk to each of them, get to know them, and hope some overarching narrative came into place, but given Urrupain's surly demeanor, Rhees' outright hostile nature, and Uche's impatience, I wasn't sure an answer of "Mind if I just hang around and poke my nose into stuff?" was going to fly. After all, outside my time in the cargo bay, Uche had been attached to my hip.

I stalled for time. "What can you tell me about the *Agapetes*?"

Uche sighed. "What do you want to know?"

"How big is she? How many crew can she accommodate? Does she have any unusual or interesting tech onboard? Engineering details, all that stuff."

"I suppose I could get you her technical specifications," said Uche.

"What about design schematics?" I asked.

"Shouldn't be a problem. Anything else?"

I was definitely detecting a note of annoyance. "I'll still need those security logs."

"I haven't had a chance to look into that yet, for obvious reasons," said Uche. "If and when I obtain those I'll pass them to Ducic."

I eyed the Tak. He stared into his wheatgrass.

"You have anything to add?" I asked.

He looked up, startled. "Pardon? Do you have need of my services?"

"What's going on? Did you nod off?" If nothing else, Ducic had remained exceptionally quiet. He'd only piped up to offer clues into his upbringing—and then been summarily shut down.

"*Nod off?* What is this expression? Was I suffering uncontrolled neck spasms of which I was not aware?"

"You seemed distracted," I said. "As if you'd fallen asleep. With your eyes open. And no, I have no idea if that's possible given your physiology."

"No. I..." He paused for a moment, took a long draught of his beverage, and set the cup on a counter adjacent to the beverage dispenser. "My apologies. I should be more focused. I suffer pangs of self-doubt, but I should not let that interfere with tasks at hand."

"Self-doubt?" I said. "Why? Because of your specialty in pseudogravitation as opposed to...I don't know, something more applicable?"

"In part, yes," said Ducic. "But also because of my upcoming year one progress evaluation. I am eager to provide my superiors with evidence of my aptitude and enthusiasm."

I lifted a brow. *Year one?* How long have you been working for InterSTELLA?"

"A little over ten standard galactic months," said Ducic. "I believe Officer Chatterjee's assignment of me to this investigation is a potentially great vote of confidence. *If* I can deliver."

I pursed my lips.

Uche stood. "Guys, could you let me escort you back to your ship? *Please?*"

"Oh. Right. Sure," I said. "*If* you get us those documents I asked for. And I reserve the right to come back and ask more questions. Not necessarily of you, but rather your crew."

"I'm sure they'll be thrilled." He waved toward the open door.

I obliged, but not before casting a surreptitious glance at Ducic. He was a *rookie?*

13

Carl met me at the airlock to the *Samus Aran,* which thankfully was still docked with the *Agapetes.* He gave me a nod. "So I got the ship schematics and technical specifications from Paige. Anything in particular you're hoping to glean from them?"

Uche had secured the documents en route to Tarja's ship and sent them to me via Brain, whereupon Paige had forwarded them to Carl. I found the speed at which he obtained and parted with the information suspicious, especially given his obvious reluctance to provide the *Agapetes'* security logs.

Ducic followed me closely, so I skirted Carl's question. "Let's look at the information together. Basically, I'm trying to get a better feel for why the *Agapetes* was targeted."

Carl and I settled ourselves onto the wraparound bench seats in the main cabin.

Ducic sidled up next to us. "Can I be of service?"

I'd kind of hoped he'd retire to his room, but I nodded. "Of course." After all, I didn't want to alienate the guy. I had a feeling we'd need him on our side if we had any hopes of unraveling the mystery presented to us.

I spotted a holoprojector above us. "Paige, can we use that to create a rendering of the *Agapetes*?"

Sure, she said. *I've got rudimentary privileges on the Samus's servenet. Don't get jealous, though. In all honesty, Tarja hasn't warmed up to me much more than she has to you.*

The projector flickered to life and a miniature version of the *Agapetes* appeared over the table.

"Perfect," I said. "Though could we get half of it displayed in blueprint form? Cut right down the middle?"

So...not perfect, said Paige. *Though I appreciate the sentiment. You know how to make a girl feel special.*

If only.

Paige obliged me, and suddenly half the ship disappeared, replaced instead with a glowing blue architectural outline showing the freighter's hold, crew quarters, maintenance shafts, engine compartments, and the rest.

"Alright, Carl," I said. "You've got the technical specifications on hand and you're better at translating schematics from digital to physical form than I am. Let's start with the crew quarters. Where are they?"

My partner stuck his index finger into a portion of the glowing blue outline. "There are two sets of two cabins. The ship is symmetrical in nature, so there's one set on each side. Each cabin can hold three humans or humanoids, for a total of twelve."

Uche had mentioned they had eight crew on board at the moment. "What about life support? It can't be designed to accommodate only twelve people."

"Of course not," said Carl. "For factor of safety reasons, it can support quite a bit more."

"How many more?"

"That's not a simple question to answer," he said. "There's no single life support system on board. Many systems work in concert to keep the ship operating at peak performance. The oxygenator and the carbon dioxide scrubbers, solid and liquid waste recycling, ship's power, heating, and magnetic field management, to name a few. The systems aren't all taxed equally by the addition of more people, and the degree to which system would be stressed is largely time dependent."

"So what you're saying is a two hour pirate attack would put a strain on the ship's oxygenators and carbon scrubbers, but not so great as to cause a problem in the long run?"

"Precisely."

I scratched my chin. I'd need Carl or Paige to run some numbers.

"Pardon," said Ducic, "but this is obvious, if not from physical calculations then from experimental evidence. Holovids clearly show attackers and crew suffering no ill effects from oxygen deprivation during attack."

"Please don't ask if I've watched the vids," I said. "I don't need anyone else questioning that for as long as we're on this case."

Ducic glanced at me with flattened ears and widened nostrils. Hopefully it wasn't an indication of his slighted honor.

I heard a thump and turned to find Tarja standing under the cockpit hatch. She sauntered over and planted her hands—now devoid of gloves—on her hips.

"So," she said. "You're back. It's a shame. I was starting to enjoy Carl's company."

I glanced at my partner. "You hit it off?"

He smiled. "I didn't say a thing."

"Hit what off?" asked Ducic.

Tarja ignored him. "I see you obtained the ships' schematics. Very nice. They're good for what exactly?"

"Gathering evidence," I said. "Putting a narrative together. That sort of thing."

"And what sort of narrative have you devised from poking at this image of the *Agapetes*?"

I tsk-tsked and shook a finger. Tarja wouldn't get any bites on this particular fishing expedition. Between the advanced warp drive tech, the pirates that seemed more like caricatures than real felons, and the clues I'd already gathered aboard the *Agapetes,* I had a general feeling about what was going on, but what if I was wrong? I didn't want to propose an unfinished theory, something Tarja or Ducic or even Carl—because I hadn't discussed it with him yet—would tear apart because of a major oversight on my part. I needed more time to think.

Tarja sighed and shook her head. "Alright, look here, Weed. I've been lenient. I brought you here on *my* ship because *you* thought it would be beneficial to interview the crew of this ship for God knows what reason. I guess because holovids aren't good enough for you. I've *tried* to be a team player—"

Haven't try very hard, said Paige.

"—but I think it's high time we cut the crap and moved onto avenues that have some chance of helping us track down these space pirates. Every minute we waste is a minute these thugs can fade further into obscurity."

"And you have a plan, I suppose?"

Tarja snorted. "Of course I do. We're going to start with recon of the asteroid belt."

I couldn't help but notice how Tarja's plan happened to keep us more or less in the same place we already were. *How convenient...* Perhaps that was why she hadn't put up much of a fuss over my initial request to head to the *Agapetes*.

"Alright," I said. "I'll bite. What exactly do you intend? To fly around aimlessly, bouncing off asteroids in the hopes one of them eventually turns out to be a pirate ship instead?"

Tarja's face tightened. "I'm a bounty hunter, you numbskull. There are hidden pirate sanctuaries built into at least a dozen asteroids in this belt. I know where they are. We'll hit them, one by one, searching for the culprits."

"I don't mean to be presumptuous," said Carl, "but that method of attack would seem to have a statistically insignificant chance of success."

"And to think I was starting to warm up to you," Tarja said. "Look. *I'm* the bounty hunter. InterSTELLA hired me for a reason. It's because I have inside knowledge of pirates, their haunts, and activities and they don't. Neither do you. So when I tell you I know where these places are, you should listen. Even if we don't find who we're looking for, we might find clues or rumors as to where they've gone."

"I wasn't doubting your credentials," said Carl. "I merely meant if the pirates were hiding under our noses, don't you think InterSTELLA's scouting expeditions would've picked up traces of their presence?"

Tarja waggled a finger. "That's where you and Vijay are wrong. What if the InterSTELLA flunkies haven't found abnormal warp signatures along the Sol-Tau Ceti line because they're looking in the wrong spots—like say, *within* the star systems? Perhaps right here in the asteroid belt."

Ducic blinked his cow eyes. "You believe said interstellar brigands are entering and exiting warp from within surrounding confines of the asteroid waistband?"

"Why not?" said Tarja. "It might sound suicidal, but these are crazed pirates we're talking about. And they clearly have advanced Alcubierre drive tech at their disposal. Perhaps for them, the exit from warp is a much more precise process than it is for us."

Ducic wrinkled his muzzle. "Precise, possibly, but it is, as a matter of physical principles, highly energetic. Should such an exit be attempted, despite level of warp drive tech, it would leave significant energy signatures."

"Precisely," said Tarja. "See? Ducic knows what I'm talking about. The belt would be a perfect place to drop out because external sensors wouldn't notice them amid the asteroids. And this plan of action gives us something else to go on. Should we somehow fail to find the pirates at their known haunts, we can roam the asteroid belt looking for warp signatures."

"I don't know," said Carl. "If you're right about any of this, it would seem a huge risk on the part of the pirates. It goes beyond leaving traceable energy signatures. I wouldn't be surprised if the warp exits vaporized asteroids in the path of their particle shock wave. All the asteroids are tracked by planetary surveys, such as those performed here on Varuna to prepare for settlement impacts. If asteroids are missing, we'd know about it."

"Who said anything about pirates being smart?" said Tarja.

That point, at least, matched my own observations from the vids, and her argument about the warp exits at least seemed physically plausible—none of which meant I thought Tarja was barking up the right tree. But I needed more time to put together my theory, and bouncing around a few asteroids would give me time to think while keeping us near the *Agapetes*.

"Fair enough," I said. "You lead, we'll follow."

Not like we have any choice, said Paige.

Ducic let out a low moan. "Very well. Should anyone need me, I will be in my quarters, partaking in sedatives and wishing for swift release from the agonies of weightlessness."

I glanced at him, then Tarja. "Does he know something I don't?"

The bounty hunter smiled. "Asteroid hopping means no constant linear acceleration. And I like to push the pace. Hope you like roller-coasters."

14

I lay on my bed, strapped into place and in the midst of rewatching one of the holovids from the attack on the *Kalanchoe,* when Paige informed me I had a visitor.

I flicked off the vid, had Paige release the straps, and sat. The ship's acceleration held me in place with a slighter force than I was used to, perhaps half a g, but at least it was constant. My stomach had hardened under the trial by fire of our asteroid avoidance maneuvers, but I hadn't yet reached Vijay's level of gastrointestinal Zen.

Tarja stood in the doorway to my quarters, a drawstring mesh bag hanging from her right hand. "Oh, thank God. You're clothed."

"Why wouldn't I be?" I narrowed an eye. "Did you walk in on Ducic unannounced and witness something you'd rather not have?"

Tarja squinted at me. "Huh? No. I... Never mind."

It dawned on me. "A joke! Sorry, you caught me of guard. If anything, I would've been less surprised if you'd kicked the door down and barreled in, ready to tear my head off with your bare hands."

"This is my ship," said Tarja. "It responds to my wishes. Why would I kick the door down?"

"That was also—" I waved my hand dismissively. "On second thought, don't worry about it. What's on your mind?"

"We're closing in on our first target. An asteroid known as TCA one three three six four nine."

"It's that special, huh?"

"The pirate bases aren't on any of the big ones," said Tarja. "That would make them easy to find."

"I'm sure it's a lifeless, uninspiring hunk of hollowed out space rock." I gave her a nod. "What's in the bag?"

She lifted the article in question. "That's why I'm here. Based upon our first meeting, I think I know the answer to this, but what's your experience in a spacesuit in zero g?"

"Let's say I'm a little rusty."

"You're not doing either of us any favors by spouting bullshit. I need to know what I'm working with."

I shrugged. "I've done it before. The spacesuit part doesn't bother me. It's the zero g I struggle with, but it's coming back, slowly but surely."

"I'd be more confident if you'd used the words *swiftly and* instead of *slowly but.*" She crossed to the built in desk, placed the sack atop it, drew open the top, and dug her hand inside. When she pulled it out, it was with a heavy pulse pistol gripped in her fist. "You ever use one of these before?"

"Hold on," I said. "Are you saying what I think you're saying? You want me to come with you into a pirate den, armed, in a spacesuit, in zero g?"

"Are you dense?" she asked. "Seriously, try to keep up, will you?"

"Why not take Carl?" I asked. "He's way better in low gravity than I am. You've seen him."

Both of Tarja's eyebrows shot up. "You want me to take a man-loving *droid* into a pirate den to back me up in case of a fight?"

"Point taken. But do you really think I'd be a better companion than nobody at all?"

"That's what I'm trying to determine," said Tarja. "As a general rule, I don't like to go after savage, blood-thirsty pirates alone."

"Because bringing a pal makes the odds so much better," I said.

"I'm telling you, the hideouts are small. I'm not expecting a crowd." Tarja approached with the pistol. "Now could you please quit screwing around and answer the question? Do you have experience firing a weapon?"

"To be honest, I have a lot more experience with hand to hand combat," I said. "I was a kick boxer once upon a time. Not that the skill translates particularly well in space."

"Seriously?" said Tarja. "You kick boxed?"

"Yeah. I was pretty good, believe it or not. But to answer your question, I have fired a pulse pistol before. Small arms training was required to obtain my private investigator's license. I even have a permit for my own weapon. Never bought one, though. I haven't had a need for it on Cetie."

"I'm assuming you trained at three, ten, and twenty-five meters. What was your contact percentage at twenty-five?"

I had to wrack my brain a bit. "About forty percent, I think?"

"Well, that's a start." Tarja held the pistol forward. "This is a standard Porter & Cunningham V5 pulse pistol. You probably used something similar, but you used it under Cetie gravity and in atmosphere. Things work different when you're in outer space. The pulse setting fires energy bursts, but it's only useful on bare skin. The pulse gets dissipated by space suits, even on the highest settings. That's by design. If we get into a jam, you'll have to operate it in projectile mode. It uses zero point five millimeter electrically charged self-expanding harpoon barbs, with a hundred barbs to a clip. Non-lethal, of course. They'll puncture a suit and deliver their charge to incapacitate the target while backfilling the entrance hole with resin. But you *have* to be aware of recoil. At two grams apiece, it might not seem like a lot, but they fire at high velocity. So don't flip out and empty your clip like some action star in a B-grade holof-lick, otherwise you're liable to find yourself flying across the asteroid belt at twenty meters per second. Got it?"

I nodded.

She handed the pistol over. "Good. Hold it. Study it. Get used to it. You've seen that circular piece of wall art in the main cabin that looks like a dart board? You can use it for target practice. We don't have a ton of time, but any preparation is better than none, and practice in a variable g environment like we're dealing with now is useful. Just be sure Ducic is in his cabin before you start. He's miserable enough as is without getting tasered."

I pressed my palm against the grip and hefted it. Because of the momentary low gravity, it felt like a feather. I'd have to get used to that. "Thanks."

"And since we're talking about low gravity space combat, there's something else I want to introduce you to." Tarja traversed back to the bag and pulled out a metal contraption, thirty centimeters long and oval-shaped. Ringed around the sides were a series of spring-loaded barbs. They looked sharp.

"These are self-driving asteroid crampons," said Tarja. "They hook into the boots of your spacesuit. They're pressure driven, with smart sensors to distinguish between artificial flooring and rock, which means they won't go off indoors. These suckers will help keep you attached to hunks of space rock like the one we're heading to, even if they only pull ten-thousandths of a g. *Help* is the operative word, though. You can't move too fast, or jump, or celebrate too hard, or pull any other dumbass shenanigans. Understand?"

I accepted the contraption. "I think I've got the general idea."

"I'd tell you to practice using the crampons," said Tarja, "but they won't work in my ship unless I took the safeties off, and if I were to do that, you'd still fail to find traction on the hard metal. And I'd have to kill you for scratching the floors up something fierce."

"Neither one of us wants that," I said. "Although now that you mention your hatred of scuffs and scratches, I'm rethinking whether or not to follow your advice about training with the pulse pistol."

Tarja smiled, but the expression faded as she realized her slip. "You've got my blessing to practice. But don't miss the target more than a half-dozen times. Otherwise I'll be forced to come up with a punishment befitting the crime. I'm thinking a non-lethal pulse round to your squishy bits."

I wanted to argue I was hard as a rock, but then I caught her meaning.

She headed for the door and paused in mid-stride. "Oh. One more thing. The suits I have are equipped with a dozen swiveling micro thrust nozzles. I highly encourage you to leave their operation up to your Brain. And don't screw around with them thinking you can go all Buck Rogers on people's asses, because the propellant they use comes from the same air supply keeping you alive. My suggestion is you only engage them if you get pushed off the asteroid into space, and even then I'd head for the ship. Think you can handle that?"

I nodded. "As snarky as she can be, my Brain has my best interests at heart. After all, if I stop breathing, things get dicey for her."

Under most circumstances, I'd be fine, said Paige. *But since I'm not actively hooked up to the Cetie servenets, you're right. Try not to die.*

I notified her I'd do my best. "So does this mean I'm coming with you?"

Tarja paused at the door. "Don't be presumptuous. We'll talk after your shooting session."

15

*T*INK.

The barb made a weak, tinny sound as it impacted the center of the target, a polymer-coated metallic shield with purple and while concentric circles drawn on its face. I'd seen it upon entering the ship and dismissed it as another piece of the décor, but upon taking it down from the wall to remove my spent barbs, I'd found the thing had a locking forearm attachment on the other side. I'd yet to see her in action, and I'd already started to theorize Tarja was more superhero than bounty hunter. It all depended on what alloy she claimed the shield was made of.

"Nice shot," said Carl. "Ready for the next?"

I bumped my head into the floor at the back of the main cabin. At first, I'd started with the basics: torso facing the target, arms squared, shots fired under constant accelerations of at least half a g. As I'd gotten more confident, I'd waited for the bumps and jostles and microgravity sessions caused by Tarja's maneuvers around asteroids. Soon, even that wasn't enough. Because of the confines of the ship, I couldn't get more than about five meters from the target, which wouldn't help refresh the precision portions of my muscle memory, but I could challenge myself in other ways. I'd made Carl apply external stimuli in the forms of pushes and pulls and rotations to get me disoriented before shooting. Even with his unpredictable antics, I'd managed to land my last ten barbs on the target, two of them dead center. I figured that was a win.

"Let's do it," I said.

Carl bounced off the floor and floated over to me, taking advantage of the current gravitational climate. He turned me to face the back wall, still keeping me upside down.

"Ready?"

"Count me down."

"Three...two...one..."

Carl spun me. The room blurred. I flicked out my arm.

Rich? Tarja.

I fired. The barb plunked into the side of the bench seats, a good meter from the target's edge.

I frowned as I responded to the Brain missive. *Yes?*

Come up to the cockpit. We're almost there.

I holstered the pistol in a shoulder carrier I'd found among the spacesuits—it was meant to go over a suit, but I'd cinched it to make it work—and headed up the hatch.

I found Tarja strapped into her chair, staring at the panoramic display—at what, I wasn't exactly sure. It looked like any other portion of the asteroid belt. Dark and empty, with the occasional far off glimmers and flashes.

"See it?" asked Tarja.

I tried to follow her gaze. There, in the center of the display, I spotted what must've caught her eye. A rock, little more than a speck at this distance, but larger and brighter than the others around us.

"Is that TCA...whatever it was?"

Tarja nodded.

I squinted. "Am I looking through the Pseudaglas directly or is this superimposed?"

"It's a display, but it's live," said Tarja. "We've got our butt facing the asteroid for the deceleration."

I floated idly toward the image. "Is there any reason you stopped us?"

"We're still closing, but at a slow constant speed. I didn't want whoever's home getting suspicious until we were on top of them."

"So there's actually pirates there?" Despite Tarja's precautionary measures, I'd expected her rhetoric to be overblown and for the place to be barren. Either that or for it to be a humming hive of scum and villainy, full of tattooed, scar-covered toughs and aliens of a dozen different races all drinking and smoking and injecting hallucinogens like in the holothriller epics.

The display zoomed in on the rock, undoubtedly in response to Tarja's Brain command, until it filled the screen. As far as asteroids went, it probably fell somewhere in the small to medium range, oblong, rocky and misshapen with a rough diameter of a few kilometers—a guess which I based on the size of the object tethered to its surface.

"Is that a...?"

"Pirate ship. Yes." Tarja held out a finger. "See that?"

For a moment, I couldn't tell what she was referring to, but as the asteroid rotated, Tau Ceti's rays caught something and sent forth a brilliant glimmer. A metal hatch, perhaps five meters across, set into the asteroid's surface.

"So they've hollowed the place out?" I asked. "To store illicit goods?"

Tarja ignored me as she unbuckled herself. "We'll be in range within a few minutes. Here's what'll happen. Once we're close I'll use the resonant cavity thrusters to ease us down, but I'll send out a harpoon to tether us to the surface. If they haven't figured out we're there at that point, they'll catch on pretty quick once they sense the harpoon. We'll drop down and maneuver toward the door using the crampons. You remember what I told you about those, right? Don't be stupid. From there we'll pry open the hatch and see what we find."

She dropped down the hatch to the main corridor, and I followed her. "So you're serious? You really think we'll find pirates?"

"Do I even need to dignify that with a response?" said Tarja. "You think someone just forgot a ship there?"

We picked up Carl in our wake as we made for the airlocks. "Okay, I'll admit that was dumb. What I meant was, what exactly do you think we're getting into? How many pirates do you think we'll find? And packing what kind of heat?"

"How the heck would I know?" said Tarja. "Do you think I'm psychic?"

I didn't, but I also didn't think the woman was being totally honest with me. After all, as Carl had pointed out, the probability of finding anyone at *any* of Tarja's super secret pirate hideouts seemed astonishingly low, yet we'd happened upon a ship at the *very first* asteroid we'd visited. What were the chances?

Tarja pointed me toward the suits as she hooked air bottles into the back of her own and strapped on a few kilos of firepower. "I monitored your shooting while I navigated us in. As you might've surmised, I think you're good enough that you won't endanger me just by being around—although I'm still not sure how you'll do in zero g on the face of an asteroid, so go slow with the crampons at first. Use exaggerated motions, and always stay behind me. If things go south in a hurry, I don't want to have to try to shoot around you. Understand?"

I shrugged into the suit, feeling it self-adjust to my thick legs and meaty neck. I still couldn't totally believe what I was about to get myself into.

Carl gave me a confident nod. "You've got this, Rich. Slow and steady." He helped me with the holster. "Remember. Use both hands for stability when firing."

Paige must've kept him abreast of my mental state, because as I snapped my helmet into place, he followed that up with, *And be careful, will you? I don't believe Tarja means us any harm, but still... I don't totally trust her.*

It was just the thing I wanted to hear before having the airlock doors snap shut behind me.

16

Silence once again enveloped me as the airlock doors opened. I stood in the mouth of the *Samus Aran,* gripping a handhold for purchase, and stared at the cold, barren expanse of rock and ice below us.

While I'd found Varuna's landscape hauntingly beautiful, the surface of the pirate's den instilled in me a chill fear. The horizon curved away perilously fast, a constant reminder of the asteroid's infinitesimal stature and negligible gravitational field. Its pockmarked grey surface had never tasted an atmosphere's breath, nor had it felt the touch of a foot or the pull of a root. It floated there, lifeless, cold, and defenseless—an insignificant speck of dust in the vast wasteland of space. And it still dwarfed me.

No offense, Rich, came Carl's familiar voice, *but if this asteroid has pirates inside it, then it has felt the touch of a foot before.*

You're still with me? I thought.

I patched him in, said Paige. *He'll see everything you do. More, actually, because he has the benefit of the ship's cameras at his disposal, as well.*

The asteroid approached. We couldn't be more than fifty meters from its surface.

So you're spying on me? I said. *Jeez. And here I thought I'd finally have some alone time to put moves on Tarja.*

Silence. I could almost picture Paige and Carl raising metaphorical eyebrows at each other. *Carl? Paige? That was a joke. Please tell me we're on a private channel.*

Don't worry, said Paige. *I granted Tarja direct access to you, but she's not privy to the rest. It's just the three of us old pals sharing your mind at the moment. And what a mind...*

You know, there's a kernel of truth to most jokes. Carl sounded worried, and not in a 'you're about to jump into the void of space to take on crazed pirates' sort of way.

I sighed. I was a hopeless romantic, but even I wasn't that bad. *I swear, I have no interest in Tarja. Even if I did, I'd probably have more success seducing a box of rusty nails.*

The end result might be more pleasurable, too, said Paige. *Though I'd recommend a tetanus shot before trying anything salacious.*

This time Carl and I stayed silent.

Oh, so you can joke about seducing an anthropomorphic icicle, said Paige, *but now I'm the one who's gone too far?*

Tarja cut in on the private feed. *Brace yourself.*

We'd closed to ten meters of the asteroid's surface. I gripped the handhold tighter.

With a shudder, the harpoon shot out from the bottom of the ship, driving itself a meter into the rock. The *Samus Aran's* resonant cavity thrusters provided a small simultaneous counter thrust, pulling the tether tight. It almost knocked me from my perch.

Tarja used the jolt to her advantage, catapulting herself onto the asteroid. Tiny chips of rock spouted from her boots as her crampons engaged the surface.

Come on in, she called to me via Brain. *The water's fine.*

Here goes nothing. I swallowed back my fear, pushed off the handle, and plunged after her.

I calculated properly, giving myself enough of a push and rotation to land lightly on my feet in a half-crouch. My confidence growing, I rose to full height and stepped forward. That's when my experience soured.

My crampons locked up. My body jerked as the force exerted through my legs crashed back through me, and I tipped forwards. As I rotated, picking up angular momentum, the crampons, sensing the torque, released, but not before putting strain on my shins. I bumped face first into the rock and rebounded, slowly floating away from the ground.

I panicked.

Don't worry, said Paige. *I've got you.*

The propellant thrusters kicked in, rotating me to a vertical position before punching me back into the rock surface.

Now, said Paige. *One foot at a time. Deliberate movements. Be sure one leg is firmly planted before moving the next.*

It sounded easy. I tried it. Turned out it was. *Huh. So not exactly like riding a hoverboard.*

Tarja cut in again. *You coming? You're not terribly useful as my backup if you hang out under the ship the whole time.*

I looked up to see her a good twenty meters ahead of me. *Hold up. If you want me close, you'll have to slow down a bit.*

Tarja kept moving. *Not happening. Not now that I'm sure the pirate scumbags know we're here. But it'll take me a couple minutes to open the hatch, so that's your chance.*

She crouched as she reached the metal doors, and I saw her grab hold of something. I hadn't asked how she intended to crash the pirate's stronghold, but as I closed on her, I saw what she held: an oversized valve handle. With each twist of the wheel, the metal hatch pulled back another few centimeters.

This sucker's mechanical? I said.

Around here, there are better things to spend your energy budget on than automatic doors, Tarja said. *Light and heat, mostly.*

So much for hacking the pirate's sophisticated hideout mainframe.

Tarja gave me a nod. *Ready your weapon.*

I pulled my pistol from its holster, making sure to attach the optional retractable wire reel to my suit's wrist first. Wouldn't want to lose it, after all. *Ready. So what's the plan? I mean, other than for me to stay behind you and follow your lead.*

Tarja wrenched on the valve handle again. *Shoot anything that moves. Even if I shoot it first. I might've missed.*

Seriously? I asked. *That's the strategy? We're not even going to try and reason with these people?*

Tarja shot me a murderous glare. *Do NOT underestimate these sons of bitches. Mercy isn't in their vocabulary. Don't even think about trying to engage them in anything but a firefight. If you do, I'll shoot you myself to get you out of the way.*

This didn't seem like the time to point back to the holovid security footage of the pirate attacks in which the pirates occasionally became violent but never crossed over to the threshold of murder, not with Tarja in the sort of mood she appeared to be in. Not that I had time to argue if I wanted. With the hatch open a good meter and a half, Tarja hopped up, disengaged her crampons, and redirected herself into the pirate base using the valve as a handle.

I followed her, though much less gracefully.

Inside the pirate den, I didn't find the humming, tightly-packed space bar I'd hoped for. It was more of a forsaken hole in the wall, except the wall in this instance was an asteroid and the hole was more literal than metaphorical. In the bright interior lighting—Tarja had been right about the energy expenditure—I could make out telltale signs of laser cutting on the rock walls, walls packed with huge bundles of space-loot trapped by adjustable cargo nets.

I didn't get a chance to inspect them properly. Tarja slammed into me, sending me flying across the room into a bundle of cargo held in the center of the bay by nets and tethers. A flurry of projectiles zipped through the vacuum my body had occupied a second prior.

It's a trap, came Tarja's voice. *One of them is on our left, aft, behind a bundle of water jugs. Lost the other one. Keep an eye out. Those projectiles aren't stun rounds.*

I pushed myself off the cargo netting, trying to orient myself. Tarja flew past. She glided across another wide bundle of tethered crates and fired off a half dozen crackling pulse rounds into a free line of sight. The momentum pushed her back, changing her trajectory mid flight. A puff of compressed air shot out her right side, flicking her behind another tethered bundle as a dozen rounds zipped by.

As I untangled my crampons from the nets, my heart starting to hammer, I couldn't help but acknowledge the bizarre majesty of a silent firefight.

I can help with that, said Paige. *Pew pew pew. See?*

Cover me, Rich, said Tarja. She launched herself down an aisle between floating boxes.

Was she insane? I hadn't signed on for this, but like the brain-addled knight in shining armor I was, I tried my best. I pushed off the netting at a ninety degree angle, readied my pulse pistol, and fired some rounds in the general direction of our shooter. The recoil from the gun sent me tilting backwards, but I was fairly sure I seriously maimed a crate of freeze-dried potato pancakes before I rotated out of sight.

Got him, said Tarja. *One down, one to go.*

I did? Guess I'm a better shot than I thought.

Not you, idiot, said Tarja. *Me.*

Oh. Well, how are you sure there's only two of them? I reached for a stray net, but I spun out of range before I could grasp it.

I've been here before, said Tarja. *This cargo hold is big, but the quarters inside aren't. I don't think the life support systems could handle more than two adult humans.*

I spun back toward the closest net. I reached out. From the corner of my eyes, I spotted a blur. It wasn't purple.

Paige activated all the thrust nozzles on the front of my suit simultaneously, rocketing me back through the cargo bay as the second pirate filled the space behind me with rounds. I slammed into another floating bundle of cargo. Thankfully whatever was inside crumpled under my blow, lessening the impact. Designer handbags and women's undergarments, based on what floated free.

Lacey though they appeared, I didn't have time to ogle them. I caught a flash of the metallic suit I'd seen moments ago. A head popped over a crate.

Paige blasted me to the side toward a free corridor, with slightly better accuracy this time. I ruined her efforts by peppering the area with more electrically-charged pulse barbs. I don't think I could've hit the broad side of an intergalactic freighter. Apparently the spike of fear and adrenaline caused by being shot at in the depths of space, where a single stray bullet would lead not only to excruciating pain but also suffocation, freezing, and rapid decompression, had a way of worsening my aim.

"Tarja! Bad guy! Ten o'clock!" I yelled. I knew she couldn't hear me, but Brain communications didn't cut it at a time like this.

Ten o'clock? What the hell does that mean? she asked.

"I don't know," I said. "He's over here. Help me!"

I've got this, said Paige. *Tarja, I'm hooking you into Rich's live feed and giving you access to everything he's seen since the start of the fight. You can superimpose it over your own visual display if you like.*

Coming, said Tarja.

I latched onto a bundle of what appeared to be spare droid parts, curled into as small a ball as possible, and held my breath.

No need for that, said Paige. *No one can hear you.*

Not the time for logic, I replied. *Life is on the line.*

Do me a favor, said Tarja. *Pop your head out, look right, and fire off a couple shots.*

Promise I won't get a bullet between the eyes?

Just do it. Now, said Tarja.

Like a good boy, I obeyed. I pulled myself up and fired a trio of shots at the wall. Seeing as our assailant wouldn't be able to hear them land, I wasn't sure what good it would do.

Apparently, he saw them land. He burst from behind a floating tethered bundle full of large metal tanks and took aim at my head.

As if in slow motion, Tarja flew out through a small shaft in the floating piles of junk, propelled by her thrust nozzles. The pirate saw her and shifted his aim. As he did so, a look of surprise washed over him, and he mouthed something.

Tarja didn't need to aim. She knew right where he was thanks to my visual feed. The split second difference afforded to her from not needing to shift her pistol made all the difference. Her shock barb slammed into the guy's chest. He shuddered and went still, his lightweight assault carbine still grasped in his hands.

Tarja holstered her pistol, rebounded off a cargo bundle, and turned to me. *I need you to drag this twitching sack of meat up to the Samus. We'll store him in your quarters. The shock barb will keep him quiet for a while, but strap him into your bed for safekeeping. I'll go rustle up the other body.*

My heart beat in my chest like a drum. *What? Seriously? That's it? No, 'Nice shooting, Tex,' or 'Glad to see you made it through in one piece,' or even a simple 'Nice job, Rich'?*

I saw Tarja sigh through her helmet, but I couldn't hear it. *Let's recap. You didn't hit a single living target in the three dozen or so rounds you shot off, you wasted a healthy portion of your air reserves gallivanting around the cargo bay like a space cowboy, and you're clearly not bleeding or venting through a projectile-inflicted hole. What do you want, a medal? Now quite whining and get this guy on the Samus.*

Tarja grabbed a nearby net and propelled herself around a batch of plastic tubs filled with something that resembled bolts. As she left, Carl's voice crackled into existence in the back of my mind. *Rich. Buddy. You forgot to put the moves on her.*

Oh shut up. I moved over toward the pirate's now still body.

Seriously, though, he said. *I, for one, am glad you're still alive. You had me gripping the edge of my seat throughout that fight, and not only because we're in microgravity.*

Thanks. I'm glad I'm alive, too.

I grabbed the pirate's arm and pulled him toward me. I glanced through his suit's helmet at the scruffy, unshaven weirdo within. The shocked expression he'd given Tarja had been frozen onto his face thanks to the electrical barb's timing.

Question, Paige.

Yes, milord?

Do you recognize this guy from the holovids?

Can't say I do.

Yeah, me neither. I cast my gaze around the cargo bay at the suspended bundles of pre-packaged food, designer clothes, cartons of nuts and bolts and ball bearings, harvested oxygenators, and RAAI Corp. surplus sexbot left arms and pinkie toes. As far as I could tell, there wasn't a single stack of iridium, platinum, tungsten, or any other heavy metal among them.

Carl still had access to my feed. *Are you thinking what I'm thinking?*

Probably, I said. *Paige, do you have the ability to send search queries through the Samus Aran back to the Cetie servenets? And to keep them hidden from prying eyes?*

I'm not sure about that last part, she said. *But I can disguise it as something else. What are we querying?*

I pressed my lips together. *I think it's time we put our collective heads together and found out who the heck Tarja Olli really is.*

17

I was looking out one of the *Samus Aran's* portholes toward the rapidly approaching surface of Varuna, my eyelids heavy, when Paige tapped me on the metaphorical shoulder.

Rich? I got something back from our Tarja query.

I blinked, instantly awake. *Yeah? Spill the beans.*

Don't get your hopes up. It's an initial report. Mostly obvious stuff culled from the public servenets. Our more complicated cross-referencing query and the stuff with the lip reading simulations won't be ready for a while yet, I'd wager.

Still. What have we got? I asked.

Well, it looks like Tarja's main qualification for this mission was...

I waited for a moment. *Don't make me beat it out of you.*

It's called a dramatic pause, said Paige, *and considering where I'm located, I'd say beating anything out of me wouldn't be a good idea. Her major qualification was...availability.*

By which you mean...?

Reports have Tarja sitting at the spaceport for a week be-fore Vijay showed up, Paige said. *As you well know, docking fees are ludicrously expensive. Word is, she was desperate for work. Bodyguard detail, escorts—with her ship, get your mind out of the gutter—really anything that would pay.*

How thoroughly did Vijay vet her? I asked.

I can't be sure, said Paige, *but based on how quickly they came to an agreement on services rendered, I'd say not very.*

That was interesting. I logged it alongside Tarja's other quirks. *And what can you tell me about Tarja's former associates?*

That's all in the expanded cross-referencing query. Sorry.

"You ready?"

I startled. Tarja had snuck up behind me. She snapped her suit's gloves into place.

"I'm good to go," I said. "Just need my helmet."

"I can tell." Tarja nodded toward my quarters. "Let's gather the cargo."

We passed Ducic's room as we headed to mine. "Heard from our InterSTELLA representative lately?" I hadn't seen him since before the asteroid raid.

"He's alive," said Tarja. "I think he's trying to sleep off his symptoms."

The door to my room puffed open, revealing the two pirates, stacked on top of each other on my bed and held in place by the straps. We'd left them in their suits, but we'd removed their helmets, otherwise they would've exhausted their air reserves long ago.

I felt a slight shudder, and my weight abandoned me. We must've finished our deceleration. Tarja undid the buckle holding the pirates down.

I grabbed one of their helmets and clipped it in place. "Is it really safe to keep them subdued under a constant electrical load like we have for the past few hours?"

"Oh, don't worry," said Tarja. "The electrical shock only knocked them out initially. They've been frozen since I shot them thanks to the neurotoxin in my barbs."

"Neurotoxin?" I blinked and shook my head. "*What?*"

"They're specially modified rounds," said Tarja. "Not totally legal in many territories. Don't tell anyone."

Tarja clipped on the other helmet and maneuvered her pirate out the door. I did the same with mine. In Varuna's microgravity, it was like carrying a sack of air.

Carl met us at the airlock and gave me a nod. "Want a hand?"

"Sure." I tossed him the pirate as I attached my helmet. "You're coming this time?"

"I don't think there's any chance of us getting involved in a firefight while we submit these fugitives to the InterSTELLA police station on Varuna," he said. "I doubt I'll get in the way."

"You're not still bitter, are you?" I asked.

"Bitter?" he said. "I was never bitter. But I'd like to point out that even if I'm not of the persuasion to engage in violent combat, I can take a bullet with the best of them."

"I appreciate that, bud, but I never got hit."

"You two ladies done? Because we've got deliveries to make." Tarja punched the airlock door shut.

I switched over to Brain communication as the pumps sucked the air from the chamber. *So, Tarja...what's the plan here?*

What are you talking about? she said. *We carry these chumps to the InterSTELLA settlement, drop them off to be picked up by the next police transport, and collect our bounties.*

Yeah, but uh... I glanced at Carl. *Have you noticed there are only two of them?*

It's obviously not the entire haul, said Tarja. *But it's a start. Enough to wet their lips. We'll work on finding the rest.*

I hadn't pushed the issue yet, mostly because I hadn't gotten the query results back from Cetie yet, but with us reaching a point of no return, I couldn't hold my tongue any longer. *Tarja, seriously. These aren't the pirates we're looking for. You have to know that.*

They're bad people. They deserve to be locked up until the end of their days, and that's a merciful fate. Do NOT question me on this.

Tone didn't come across well in Brain missives, but I could see Tarja's face through her helmet. I knew when to keep my mouth shut.

The exterior airlock door snapped open, and we hopped out lightly onto Varuna's dusty surface. We'd parked the *Samus* in a designated landing area, a fair ways from the InterSTELLA settlement at the foot of the strip mine, but thanks to the low gravity we closed the gap in a handful of buoyant jumps. It was surprisingly fun. Made me want to abandon pirate hunting for the day and test my skills at low gravity aerials. Instead, I put on my grown-up hat and followed Tarja's lead. She'd notified the InterSTELLA police about our cargo and told them we'd be heading their way.

Paige tinted my visor as we approached the gleaming metallic structure. The glare was blinding, making it so I couldn't even make out the blinking red light above the nearest airlock. Luckily Tarja knew where to go—or at least her Brain did.

A new voice cut in as we arrived at the exterior door. *That's close enough. InterSTELLA officer Brady. You three the bounty hunters?*

Technically, me and my pal Carl are private investigators, I said.

Tarja cut us off. *That's right.*

And you said you had two charges? said the officer.

I sent over a package with the details I skimmed from their computers on TCA 133649, said Tarja. *Did you not go through it?*

Silence reigned, during which I imagined the officer on the other side cursed Tarja's very existence.

Eventually he responded. *It's here. Look, I've got an incoming transmission from HQ I have to take. I'm opening up the exterior doors. Hop in and I'll start the cycle.*

The doors slid open and we entered. I looked at Tarja. *You skimmed data from the pirates' computers?*

What? she said. *I told you they were bad dudes.*

I'm more concerned about what you haven't told me, I said.

A new voice cut in, one I hadn't expected or even known was in our comm channel. *Pardon, compatriots. This is Ducic. Are you receptive of my missives?*

The doors closed behind us and air hissed as it began to fill the chamber. *We hear you. Good to know you're alive and well.*

Alive, yes, but perhaps not so well. Due to microgravity, I feel as if my arterial valve has closed to a fifth of its natural girth. My breath is heavy, and despite the presence of neural sedatives coursing through my veins, I can barely—

What do you want, Ducic? asked Tarja.

I could envision the Tak's nostrils widening. *Of course. My wellbeing is of minimal concern. I bring only news of a missive relayed to me from the Snowbell.*

Being? asked Tarja.

Word has arrived via freighter from the Sol system, said Ducic. *A sixth attack has occurred.*

18

I settled myself on the wrap-around bench seats in the *Samus Aran's* main cabin. Tarja took a seat across from me. I'd shrugged out of my suit, but Tarja had kept hers on as a force of habit—minus the helmet and gloves, of course. She glared at me, but she'd lost some of her ferocity over the past twenty minutes. I glared right back. Unlike her, my rage had only been building.

Carl joined us, leading Ducic to the table in the low gravity. The latter's eyes glazed over and his ears lay listless against his skull, but other than that, he didn't look particularly out of sorts. Of course, he was covered in fur, so even if his physiology allowed him to become pale or flushed, I wouldn't notice. Carl sat next to me while Ducic steadied himself against the table with his rudimentary hands.

"Ducic," I said. "Good to finally see you outside your room. How are you holding up?"

"I believe I understand the crux of your query," he said, "and while the true answer shows me in a less than glamorous manner, I believe social convention among your species is to don a mask crafted from flayed skin cells of a courageous adversary and build a ruse of wellbeing."

"The phrase 'put on a brave face' doesn't have such gruesome origins," I said. "Either way, I'm sorry to hear you're not feeling any better. But we need to discuss our plan of action, and I thought you should be present to provide your insight."

"Look," said Tarja. "Before we start, can I just say—"

"I think you've said quite enough for the time being," I snapped.

"I get it, you're upset," said Tarja. "But I wasn't lying. Those pirates are the scum of the cosmos. Based on what we found in their cargo bay, they've been hitting InterSTELLA ships for months. At *least*. The officers here on Varuna wouldn't have accepted them into their brig if I hadn't been able to prove that with the files skimmed from their computers."

"None of which is an excuse," I said. "Those pirates aren't *the* pirates we're after. You took advantage of an expenses-paid InterSTELLA contract to pursue some sort of personal vendetta, for God knows what reason."

"Are we here to discus theology? If so, I am woefully unprepared."

"Can it, Ducic," I said, keeping my gaze trained across the table. "You wasted all of our time, Tarja. You lied to us, and you put me personally in harm's way for your own personal gain. What part about that whole 'we're a team' spiel that I delivered in your office did you not understand?"

Tarja matched my gaze, but her visage wasn't as hard as it had been. "As I said, I get it, but I've been after those two bastards for a long time. I would've gone after them sooner if I could've, but I needed the SEUs from the InterSTELLA contract, and I really did feel more comfortable with you as backup. When you suggested coming to the asteroid belt, I figured why not take a shot?"

"You figured wrong." I paused and took a measured breath. "But...I meant what I said earlier. We need to work together as a team. I'm willing to grant you a mulligan, and not only because you're the one with a ship. There are few enough of us as it is, and we won't be able to unravel this without everyone pitching in. As I see it, this most recent pirate attack is a blessing. It means the pirates are still active, and with any luck, we'll be able to track them down before they disappear into the dark of the cosmos."

"Fine," said Tarja. "From now on, no more vendettas or personal agendas. I'm on board with the mission. I give you my word."

I glanced at the Tak. "Ducic?"

He blinked. "Am I being asked to assert my loyalty? I do not know if this is meaningful. I am already sworn by oath to uphold the values and best interests of Inter-STELLA, including but not limited to—"

"Good enough," I said. "Lets get down to brass tacks—by which I mean we should talk business. Everyone's watched the holovids of the attacks, right?"

"I should've known you'd had a theory to share," said Tarja. "Let's have at it, then. Lay it on me."

To Ducic's credit, he didn't interrupt with an inane questions about the meaning of either turn of phrase.

"Here's the way I see it," I said. "I've watched all those holovids from start to finish, some of them more than once, and I've taken away a number of observations. Namely, the pirates are disciplined. Efficient. They have an impressive team of loader bots at their disposal. They're good shots with their pistols, and they follow orders. But they also tell dirty jokes and laugh when their friends fall down. They wear dopey color-coordinated outfits and carry stun pistols exclusively. Their captain, an effusive, charismatic fellow, seems to have a bit of a mean streak to him, and yet neither he nor any of his men have killed a single one of the crew of the ships they've attacked."

"And?" said Tarja. "Where are you going with this?"

"That's the thing, isn't it?" I said. "It doesn't paint a cohesive narrative when you put it all together. There have been firefights between the attacking pirates and the crew members on several of the ships, but no casualties, other than the vented airlock on the *Agapetes*. Compare that to our experience today. The pirates we encountered on TCA whatever it was didn't chat us up or demand our worldly possessions or try to stun us. They tried to kill us, with live ammo. From what I've been led to believe, that's the more common approach. Dead men tell no tales, as the saying goes. So why is Captain Horatio and his crew so merciful?

"And another thing. The pirates' mysterious warp tech. I don't know about you, but when I watch the vids, I don't see physicists and mathematicians and scholars. I don't see anyone who could've developed that level of technology on their own. As efficient as the crew may be, they don't strike me as the sort who could infiltrate and rob a facility that *would* have the sorts of physicists and engineers who could create said advanced warp drive technology. And *if* that technology were to have been developed and fallen into the wrong hands, I get the feeling whoever developed it, whatever their intentions of secrecy may have initially been, would've come forth by now."

"I disagree with that final statement of fact," said Ducic. "Such a technology would be inordinately valuable, and owners of said technology might not even know of its loss. But I do comprehend your general sentiment. You doubt overall plausibility of the purported technology."

"Exactly," I said. "And if you eliminate the impossible, whatever's left, however improbable, must be true."

"I do not fully understand this euphemism of yours," said Ducic, "but I must combat your final conclusion. If technology for intercepting and matching warp bubbles does not exist, then how were brigands able to dock to InterSTELLA freighters in the middle of their warp trajectories?"

I smiled. "The better question is, is there a pirate ship *at all*?"

Tarja glanced at Ducic and then back at me. "This is why you needed the *Agapetes'* schematics, isn't it?"

"Bingo. Paige, bring those up."

My Brain dominatrix obliged. The holoprojector flicked into action, displaying the same half solid, half outline version of the *Agapetes* as before. "The ship's architectural schematics are telling, but I'm getting ahead of myself. The first clue that caught my eye was what *wasn't* in the holovids. For one thing, vids were only provided from the start of each attack until the end, a couple hours at most. Am I correct about that, Ducic?"

He nodded. "I provided you with all vids I myself was given."

"And the vids, while thorough, had gaps in coverage," I said. "The biggest being surveillance of the airlocks. None of the attacked ships have holorecorders in the airlocks, or at the very least, that footage wasn't provided to us. Similarly, the holorecorders in the cargo bay are positioned so you see into the bay toward the ship, not out the doors. That alone didn't make me suspicious, but when Ducic told me external ship's surveillance hadn't detected the presence of the pirate ship—due to the presence of the warp bubble, to be fair—that piqued my interest."

I poked the projection of the *Agapetes* with my finger. "So I thought, what if the pirates could've hidden themselves aboard the ship prior to takeoff? As you can see from the schematics, there simply isn't space aboard to do that. The best place to hide would be in the cargo bay itself, but that space stays evacuated throughout the trip. And, of course, if the pirates had been hidden on the ship, why would the vids show them entering the *Agapetes* through the airlock? The answer is obvious. The whole thing was staged."

Ducic looked at me with flattened ears. "I beg forgiveness. I do not understand."

"He believes the theft was an inside job," said Tarja.

"Think about it," I said. "There's no place on board the *Agapetes* to *hide* three dozen pirates, but they could fit. They'd have to sleep in the break room and the engine room and on the floors of corridors, but the ship could handle them. Carl did the math. The life support systems could support that many people, at least for a trip of the duration between a Sol-Tau Ceti jump."

"So let me get this straight," said Tarja. "You think the crew of the *Agapetes* was in cahoots with a gang of pirates who they let onto their ship. When the time was right, the pirates packed themselves into the airlocks, came out firing, and took down the crew, all of which was a farce so they could split the profits from their attack. And that this happened on a grand total of six different ships, with six different crews—meaning this group of pirates are not only great actors, but extremely well connected."

"I didn't say it was likely," I said. "But as I said—if you remove the impossible from the equation, the improbable must be considered. And I'm not basing this on the mere possibility of it from a life support standpoint. Consider again the pirates' merciful nature. Heck, don't just consider it. Watch the holovid of Captain Horatio in the *Agapetes*' command center. Do Captain Rhees, or Uche, or any of the others really seem that scared? They're defiant, but not fearful. Even Wilkins, who takes a beating, doesn't seem squeamish. Perhaps because he knew Horatio would deal him a few swift blows and no more."

"I remember the vid, and I get where you're coming from," said Tarja, "but right off the top of my head, I can think of two *major* problems with this theory, and I'm not even talking about the sheer testicular fortitude it would take to pull off a concerted effort of that magnitude six times in a row. First off, why would Wilkins vent a few of the pirates into space if they were on the same side, and, oh yeah, *where the heck did all that cargo go if there wasn't a pirate ship?*"

"Good points," I said, "and while I don't have answers to either, I've come up with some theories. First, Wilkins and the spaced pirates. It's possible they were victims of a malfunction, or a door actuator broke during the pirates' raid as a result of an errant pulse shot, causing their evacuation to the cargo bay. Honestly, I don't think that theory holds much water. What seems more likely is that their deaths were deliberate. Maybe the pirates who died had started to voice their concerns over the raids, were angling for a change in leadership, and Captain Horatio found out. In either case, the remaining pirates and crew would've had to hide the reasons for killing those pirates to protect the overall ruse. Hence, Wilkins' beating—and why it wasn't worse than it was."

Tarja rolled her eyes. "I suppose that's *plausible*, however unlikely. But what about the cargo?"

"Well, as I see it, there are two possibilities. The cargo could've been shifted outside the ship but still within the warp bubble—which shouldn't be that difficult given the Alcubierre drive compresses space time, leaving the ship itself at rest. Without accelerative forces, the cargo would stay at zero gravity and in place outside the hold. After the staged raid was complete, they could move the cargo back onboard, and move it off the ship by conventional means upon completion of the warp thrust."

Ducic wrinkled his muzzle. "I do not trust this assumption. Warp bubble adheres tightly to ship's shape. Moving so much cargo outside ship's hold while keeping it in bubble would be most difficult. Perhaps impossible."

"Can the bubble be enlarged?" I asked.

Ducic regarded the holoprojection. "I suppose. Alcubierre engine is not tailored to each ship. It is mass produced for freighters, some larger than the *Agapetes*. If bubble were enlarged, however, it would consume more energy during burn. Said energy consumption would undoubtedly show in ship's logs."

"One more thing to ask of Captain Rhees, then," I said.

"You said you had another theory?" said Tarja.

"Yes. It's possible the pirates tossed the cargo into the warp bubble itself."

"*What?*" Tarja lifted an eyebrow. "Why would they do that? *Can* you even do that?" She eyed Ducic.

The Tak nodded. "Again, this is physically possible. It would atomize cargo, however, and also leave anomalous signatures in ship's energy expenditure logs."

"So why would anyone do it?" asked Tarja.

"Well, it's a stretch," I said, "but InterSTELLA is a publically traded company. As far as I can tell, they've kept this whole pirate thing under wraps for the time being, but it'll come out soon enough. When it does, the fallout could be severe. Maybe someone's shorting the company's stock."

Tarja snorted. "Are you serious? Come on. This is beyond ludicrous."

"Is it?" I asked. "Then why have the *Agapetes'* crew been so cagey around us? I still haven't gotten the security logs I requested from Uche. How do you think he and Rhees will respond when we ask for an energy usage report from the Alcubierre drive? And I haven't even mentioned the most glaring oddity about this whole investigation."

"Which is?" asked Tarja.

"The three of us," I said. "Think about it. Ducic is a rookie who's barely been on the job ten months, and his area of expertise is in pseudogravitation, not warp bubbles. I'm inexperienced, to say the least. Prior to this hire, I'd had only one meaningful case, and to be completely honest, I resolved that mostly through luck. I've never investigated anything off Cetie before. Which leaves you, Tarja."

Her face hardened. "What about me?"

Paige still hadn't gotten the full search results back, so I wasn't entirely sure what her deal was. I improvised. "Well, as skilled as you are, you're one woman. You're expected to bring down a group of three dozen trained pirates? It's not like Ducic's or my addition tilts the scales much in our favor."

Ducic tilted his head, his nostrils wide. Perhaps he hadn't liked my assertion of his inexperience. "What is your insinuation?"

"I'm saying we were set up to fail. Doesn't anyone else find it odd Vijay hasn't bothered to keep in touch? That he placed us in Ducic's care and cast us on our merry way? If I'm right and this is an inside job, then it goes beyond the walls of the *Agapetes*. It has to, seeing as six ships have been hit. Someone's trying to make sure nobody outside InterSTELLA finds out what's going on. That's why our motley crew was selected to conduct the external investigation."

Tarja and Ducic glanced at each other. While I couldn't read the Tak, I could tell I'd struck a nerve with the former.

"Okay, Rich," said Tarja. "I'm interested, but if you're right, this is going to be extremely hard to prove. And we can't trust anyone on the inside." She glanced at Ducic, but I didn't think he picked up on the insinuation. "So what do you propose?"

"Most importantly, we need to gather more evidence." I smiled. "Thankfully, the place to do that is right next door."

19

The airlock door blinked open, revealing Uche Jones standing with his hands on his hips at the intersection of the *Samus Aran* and the *Agapetes*. He frowned.

"You don't have to look quite so happy to see us," I said. "What will your superiors think?"

"Spare me the wit," he said. "I've been up for almost twenty-five standard galactic hours, and I'm not in the mood for it."

Now that he mentioned it, the skin under his eyes did seem baggy. "That busy, huh?"

"No," he said. "I'm voluntarily taking part in a study that aims to test how sleep deprivation affects the mood of people who have to deal with aggravating twits."

"Sorry," I said, holding my hands up for peace. "Just trying to do our jobs. You received our request?"

He stifled a yawn. "Remind me."

Tarja stepped forward. "The droid and I need to check your engine compartment. Talk to one of your engineers—Watkins or that woman with the short hair—and get the logs to check for any anomalies in the various ship's systems."

"And I was hoping to talk to the rest of the crew," I said. "Ducic will accompany me. He understands physics better than I do, so he can ask the questions I'm too ignorant to."

"Fine. Whatever," said Uche. "Ms. Olli, come with me. You remember how to get to the break room, right Mr. Weed? Wait there with Ducic and I'll send over who I can. But don't expect their dispositions to be any sunnier than mine. We're all busting ass to get this ship off the ground on schedule." He waved for Tarja and Carl to follow him.

I called out to him as he walked away. "I still need those security logs, you know."

"It's out of my hands," he said without turning back. "Captain Rhees knows you need them. She'll send them your way if and when she gets to it."

If and *when*. Rhees must've been the ringleader. She was the ship's captain after all, but she'd have the knowledge, wherewithal, and ability to change the security logs to her pleasing. I wasn't hopeful for getting anything of use out of those after she was done with them, but I had to try.

Ducic followed me as I headed in the direction of the break room. "So, Rich, seeing as we have not yet discussed it, what is our plan of assault in regards to questioning of the *Agapetes'* crew?"

We're not going to question the crew, I sent him via Brain. *At least, that's not our primary goal.*

"It's not?" he said.

Brain communication only from now on, I said. *Private channel. Encrypted. We don't want prying ears to hear.*

Why not? asked Ducic.

Come on, Ducic. Stick with me, I said. *We can't trust any of them. Anything they tell us is liable to be lies. We're here for evidence of the pirates' presence.*

Such as?

I passed the door to the break room and kept right on going, heading in the direction of the crew quarters, as based on the schematics I'd received.

Anything, really, I said. *We saw the items in the evidence locker aboard the Snowbell. Pulse pistols, clothing or scraps thereof, multitools, cutting flares, that sort of thing. Plus anything that indicates there were large numbers of people on the ship for an extended period of time. Don't ask me what that could be. Portable carbon dioxide scrubbers or bedrolls for all I know.*

We hooked a right down a long hallway and passed an open maintenance hatch that spewed lukewarm air—probably a conduit to the engine compartment and the ship's compact fusion reactor, which produced a little more heat than needed when parked. Ducic's hooves echoed off the corridor floor, cutting through the omnipresent hum of the ship's electronics and life support systems.

We arrived at the first shared bedroom. Luckily, the door opened at my approach. I was worried they were programmed only to act for authorized crew members.

Ducic paused as I stepped through the portal. *Rich. I am conflicted about propriety of this action. We assured first mate Jones we would wait in the break room.*

I took a look around the cozy quarters. A pair of bunks took up half the far wall, neighbored by a set of thin doors I assumed contained the occupants' garments. Another bed was built into the near wall and flanked by a desk. At my left, two plush chairs sat under a holoprojector, tilted slightly toward one another to provide an illusion of intimacy.

Ducic, come on, I said. *You agreed we needed to look into the theory I presented aboard the Samus. How are we supposed to find evidence of the pirates' presence without a little snooping?*

I understand, said Ducic, refusing to enter the room. *But we are aboard an InterSTELLA vessel and acting against the wishes of, if not necessarily express command of, a ship's captain. I forgive you for your ignorance, but in space, a captain's mandate is akin to rule of law.*

I was about to point out we weren't in space, at least not technically, when Paige butted in on my private channel. *Before you go saying anything you regret, Rich, remember we need Ducic. You remember Vijay's statements about his clearance? He's the only contact we have who can provide insider InterSTELLA information—unless you plan on relying on Vijay, that is.*

Paige knew I didn't. Though I was mostly certain of Ducic's ignorance and innocence, at this point, I didn't trust Vijay further than I could throw him—on Cetie, not in outer space.

Fine, I told Ducic. *I won't ask you to do anything you're not comfortable with. Just keep an eye out, will you?*

You are capable of such a feat? asked Ducic. *It sounds painful.*

Just watch the hall, will you?

I opened the nearest wardrobe door and took a peek inside. Nothing but petite-sized blue engineer's uniforms, perhaps belonging to the woman with the pixie cut. A few different pairs of shoes, all designed for function rather than form, populated the bottom. Of parti-colored scarf burka do-rag thingamajigs, however, there were none. I popped open the adjacent wardrobe door, but it, too, held nothing more than uniforms and shoes.

I soldiered on to the drawers beneath, where besides socks and undergarments—which I declined to touch—I found a number of personal items: snack bars, individually-wrapped chocolates and flavor crèmes, tubes of hand lotion guaranteed to prevent cracking from dry, reoxygenated air, cosmetics, a handheld floating Blaster Dodger™ sphere the likes of which I hadn't seen in about forty years, and a vintage leather-bound digital reader. Apparently, one of the crew preferred to cozy up with a real screen rather than read their books via Brain. It's what I didn't find that disappointed me. No remnants of the pirate gang, so far as I could tell.

I stood and tapped my chin with my index and middle finger. As I did so, I heard the distinctive trill of a Brain call.

Who's that? I asked Paige.

Captain Rhees. I swear I heard a hint of guilt in her voice.

Ignore her.

The trill continued. *That may not be such a good idea, Rich.*

I moved to the far bunk. The trill stopped only for the speakers in the ceiling to come alive with the Captain's stern voice. "Weed. What the hell are you doing?"

"Oh, hey, Captain." I lifted the pillow from the bunk and looked underneath. Nothing. "Sorry. I was looking for the bathroom and got lost."

"And you thought you might find it under ensign Kass's pillow?"

"I've relieved myself in worse places," I said.

"Cut the shit. Did you think I wouldn't notice you bumbling around my ship like a Dirax caught in a solar flare? First mate Jones instructed you to go to the break room and wait there for the access to my crew that you requested."

I took a last quick look around the room. Could there be anything incriminating in the desk drawers? "Yes, I know. Again, apologies. If you could just point me toward the restroom..."

Ducic bleated through the open doorway, but to his credit he didn't enter. "Captain Rhees! This deception was not born of my free will. It is of Rich's doing. He chose to infiltrate your ship's underbelly in search of clues. Please do not report this indiscretion in logs for my performance review."

I rolled my eyes. What a pal...

The door to the room closed shut with a puff, trapping me inside.

Captain Rhees' voice came back through the speakers. "Alright, Weed, I don't know what you're up to, and I don't care. I told you I don't tolerate nonsense of any sort on my ship, and I meant it. You and your team's permissions to be on board the *Agapetes* have been summarily revoked. I'm sending Urrupain down there to escort you back to your craft. He's not typically good-natured, but I've told him to be gentle, so if he shoots you for insubordination, that's on you."

"What?" I said. "Come on. Look, I'm sorry. I shouldn't have wandered off, but I got bored. What happened to obeying your superiors? I thought you'd been ordered to assist us in our investigation."

"Why do you think you're being escorted to your ship and not to our brig?"

I took a deep breath and sighed. So much for my investigative efforts. I eyed the desk and its drawers. I was locked in the room, after all...

Restraint won over as I sat down in one of the plush chairs. Rhees still had time to change her mind, after all.

20

To Captain Rhees' credit, she might not have been quite as heartless and conniving as I'd envisioned her as I sat there in the *Agapetes'* crew quarters. She'd come through with the security access logs, including door access, and she'd provided us with the records of all the ship's internal measurements and readings, not just Alcubierre drive function and energy draws.

That made me suspicious of my own theory, but just because she'd provided the information didn't mean she hadn't tampered with it first.

I sat on the central bench seats of the *Samus Aran's* main cabin, strapped in to avoid floating off during our intermittent periods of zero gravity. Ducic had retreated to his room to go over the various technical reports concerning the *Agapetes'* engine and warp drive while Carl and I had concerned ourselves with the security logs. Tarja, wanting no part of either of those tasks, had confined herself to the cockpit, where she was in the process of navigating us hither and thither around the

asteroid belt, scanning the empty space between floating hunks of rock for warp exit signatures. Apparently,
she still liked her theory of pirates dropping out of
warp among the planetoids to avoid detection—which
wasn't a bad idea, but it assumed the pirates had advanced tech at their disposal, and I'd made my position
on that clear. Not that I'd found evidence to support my
claim. *Yet*.

I scrolled through the access logs via Brain, but I
wasn't sure how much I got out of them. Despite my
prior stint as a Brain app designer—a very *short* stint, I
might add—I was never good with code. It all seemed
like gibberish. Ones and zeros. Hexadecimals. Double
less than signs and close brackets. Backslashes and co-
lons. Abbreviations. Lots and lots of abbreviations. And
so many numbers. Over and over. Scrolling by, endlessly. Scrolling endlessly. Scrolling...

"Rich?"

I startled and blinked. My chin felt wet, as did a
patch of my collar.

Carl tilted his head. "Were you napping?"

"What? Me?" I wiped away the drool with my forearm. "No way. Too focused on the task at hand. So...find
anything?"

Carl gave me a dubious look, but he was too polite to
say anything. If anything, he probably *wanted* me to nap,
but I'd mostly stopped partaking in those eighty years
ago.

"Yes and no," said Carl. "I've found the snippets
within the logs that track the opening of the cargo bay
doors, as well as the airlock doors. The problem is,

there are no anomalies. As far as I can tell, the *Agapetes'* security wasn't hacked."

"Which supports my theory that the crew opened the doors voluntarily," I said.

Carl shook his head. "That's the rub, though. The logs show the doors opening, but they don't have a trail showing where those commands originated. If the commands came via Brain, there should be a trail, and there isn't."

"And *that* supports my theory that someone tampered with these logs before delivering them to us." I snapped my fingers. "Dang, I'm good."

Carl pursed his lips. "I don't know, Rich. That's a careless solution. Heck, providing us with these logs alone is a poor idea for someone who might be trying to hide their involvement."

"So you *don't* think anyone tampered with the access logs?"

Carl shrugged. "Maybe, maybe not. If I were doing it, I would've done it differently, assuming I wasn't rushed. The way it's presented, the logs make it seem as if the doors just...opened."

"By the hand of God?" I said.

"Your guess is as good as mine. There's precious little about this case that makes any real sense."

Rich?

Yes, Paige? I thought.

I got back another of our queries from the Cetie servenets.

I sat up. *On Tarja?*

No, the more recent one you had me send. To gather whatever information we could on the pirate attacks.

Oh. I slouched back into the seat. *It feels as if I just instructed you to send that one.*

You did, more or less, said Paige. *The search took almost no time at all. If not for transit lag, we would've had the results instantly.*

That sounds ominous.

You're not as dumb as you look, Paige said. *The query brought up nothing. No mention of recent InterSTELLA pirate attacks. Certainly nothing public.*

I looked at Carl.

He'd been following along. "This isn't surprising. Vijay said the matter had been retained internally. If you hope to find anything, you'll need to access Inter-STELLA's private servenets."

And you know who we need for that, said Paige.

The door at the far side of the room puffed open, and Ducic trotted out.

"Speak of the devil," I muttered under my breath. Then, in a louder voice, "Ducic! You're looking chipper. Feeling any better?"

He waved with his stunted arm and came over. "Marginally. Perhaps this loss and gain of apparent gravity due to our intermittent acceleration and deceleration is causing my body to undergo a 'jury by incineration,' as you would say. I no longer feel at brink of death. My demise is merely at arm's length."

Given the length of his arms, I wasn't sure how much of an endorsement that was. "Well, I...guess that's good. The improvement, anyway."

"Hopefully your improved disposition has made it easier for you to focus on your work," said Carl.

Ducic nodded. "You are curious about my delving into the engine and drive reports. I am pleased to admit I have made progress, though not as much as I would under conditions of constant gravitation." His ears flattened slightly. "You may, however, be displeased with my results."

"Why?" I asked. "Don't tell me you weren't able to find any anomalous readings."

"On the contrary," said Ducic. "I detected said anomalies, but I am unable to provide a confirmation of your theories."

"Go on."

"I isolated energy flux parameters for Alcubierre drive function during the pirate attack and found significant fluctuations in engine's power draw. Severe spikes and dips in consumption. Said fluctuations could be caused by a number of factors. One could be disposal of cargo into warp bubble, as you theorized. Similar readings would be caused by atomization of mass on exterior of bubble, but probability of this occurring is statistically nil, especially in well-travelled Sol-Tau Ceti corridor. However—I cannot rule out what sort of fluctuations would be caused to Alcubierre drive's energy draw if external bubble were to interact, or merge, with the *Agapetes'* bubble."

"I'm not sure what the problem is," I said. "It sounds like you're saying my theory has legs."

"I am not remarking on the ambulatory nature of your theory," said Ducic. "I am merely stating what you proposed *may* be feasible, although nothing about data would specifically support your assumption. Another negative point I can convey is related to overall energy draw of drive throughout warp thrust. As I can tell, the draw is in line with traditional parameters that would be expected from a vessel of this size. Perhaps a little high—though this may be due to an inefficiency in drive itself or a fault in my calculations. I am, after all, an expert in pseudogravitation. But data indicates warp bubble was not expanded sufficiently to accommodate for storage of cargo external to ship."

"So perhaps the pirates didn't steal the cargo for the cargo's sake," I said. "I've already accounted for that possibility."

And that possibility, even more so than the other one, paints InterSTELLA in a light that's shady as all get out, said Paige to me. *By the way, don't forget to ask Ducic about running a search on InterSTELLA's internal servenets.*

I'll get there.

The ship lurched and whatever sense of gravity we'd had abandoned us. Even with the practice I'd received, I felt my heart rise into my throat. Ducic gripped the table for support, and his eyes widened.

I gave my partner a nod. "Carl, can you head to the cockpit to see how long Tarja plans on keeping this up?"

"You're sending *me* into the lion's den?"

"I get the feeling she doesn't dislike you as much as me," I said. "Probably because you're inherently kind and subservient."

Carl gave me a look that indicated he didn't expect his trip to do any good, but he floated off toward the hatch nonetheless.

Ducic's nostril's flared, and I thought he might hurl—at least until I remembered he wasn't physically able.

"You alright?" I asked.

"I will persist." He didn't look particularly sure of himself.

"I imagine this is why you chose to study pseudogravitation." I shook my head. "I don't know why Tarja is insistent on roaming the asteroid belt looking for warp signatures. Seems like a complete waste of time to me."

Ducic's tongue lapped over the tip of his muzzle. "Despite my abhorrent reaction to these gravitational conditions, I understand her course of action. Her search efforts are not hindering us from performing our own analyses of data gathered from the *Agapetes*—at least not more than I have already mentioned in regards to my malady—and her theory about pirates exiting from warp *does* have merits."

"You think I'm wrong, then? You think the pirates *do* have advanced Alcubierre drive tech?"

"I do not know, Rich," said Ducic. "But I must admit—as possible as your theories regarding said pirates seem, they are not particularly plausible. They require jumps of faith, as you would say. If we assume instead a single leap, that of superior technology on part of our assailants, the assaults make sense. For example...well, I digress. Technical discussions do not interest you."

"Why would you say that?"

"Because of your disposition when subject was previously broached," said Ducic. "You asked for a 'rain check,' which I have since come to understand is a euphemism for complete and total disinterest in a subject."

"What?" I said. "No. Come on, I was serious. I'd love to talk shop with you."

Ducic's ears perked, and his death grip on the table eased. "For truth?"

"Yes, of course. I value your opinion. Let's talk physics, and engineering for that matter. I may not understand it all, but if you have theories about how the pirates might be doing what they're doing—even if it conflicts with my hypotheses—I'm all ears."

Ducic's eyes narrowed.

"It means I'm listening and paying attention."

"Ah. Thank you," said Ducic. "Well, to your point, I am unable to provide insights into the engineering required to modify an Alcubierre drive to match needs of pirates, but I have thought about physical requirements of such a device. Most glaring is a need for space-time precision."

"What do you mean by that?" I said.

"At first I was convinced matching trajectories of ships in mid-warp would be impossible given our current understanding of physical principles, mainly based on the conundrum of detection. As I have mentioned, light cannot penetrate a warp bubble, which means traditional sensing methods cannot be used to track motion of a ship within said bubble. How, then, would anyone know where a ship within a bubble *is*, much less match its trajectory?

"But your theory of pirates possessing a connection to someone at InterSTELLA—how would you say?—hit my nerve endings. What if pirates have access to Inter-

STELLA navigation logs? We pride ourselves on keeping detailed spatial coordinates of all ships that enter and exit warp. It is a necessity to make sure warp bubbles between passing ships do not interact. But what if an interaction was intended? A party armed with knowledge of ships' trajectories could follow one of our ships, use a more powerful warp burst to catch said ship, and match compression and expansion parameters to bring itself alongside ship in question. It would be incredibly difficult, but only real barrier is *precision*."

"*Precision?*" I parroted.

Ducic stopped himself. "Well, that is incorrect. Many other barriers exist. One would have to match warp bubble oscillation frequency between ships, which is theoretically possible but difficult in practice due to varying mass-energy requirements between ships of different sizes. And there are, of course, extreme energy requirements necessary to compress space time in an infinitesimal plane opposing two ships' perpendicular expansion vectors. And that is without giving consideration to how space time would be affected outside the bubble. That level of compression could lead to anomalous temporal modes even *within* warp bubble."

"Anomalous temporal modes?" I said. "I thought warp drives only affected space time *outside* the bubbles."

"Incorrect," said Ducic. "Effects are measureable both within and without. The greater the compression, the greater the space time fluctuations. In fact, I should check ship's chronometer logs to check for inconsistencies against the total warp duration as measured by stationary probes at warp entrance and exits."

I tapped my fingers on the table and lifted an eyebrow. "Good point. I was about to mention that myself."

"Were you?" said Ducic. "Then we are of like minds. Apparently you possess a keener understanding of physical sciences than I expected from your previous utterances."

Sarcasm was lost on him, but better for him to think I was smarter than I really was.

"Pardon, Rich," said Ducic as he released the table, "but I must return to my quarters. This discussion of ours, as one-sided as it was, has aroused in me new patterns of thought. I would like to grant them my focused contemplation."

"No problem." Paige poked me as Ducic began to turn. "But one thing, before you go. I was hoping you could run a search for me on the InterSTELLA servenets."

"Of course," said Ducic. "What for?"

"Anything and everything you can get on the pirate attacks," I said. "And not the stuff available to all employees. We need the classified materials, too. I want to know the entire chain of command. Who's telling who to do what, who's investigating which attacks, that sort of thing."

"I do not anticipate this to be problematic," said Ducic. "For a friend such as you, Rich, I would be happy to."

A *friend?* Dang. Was that how Ducic saw me? I had to admit, the guy was growing on me, too.

"I appreciate it, Ducic," I said, "but let's not get cocky. If I'm right about there being a mole somewhere in InterSTELLA, we need to be careful. Don't push the limits of your clearance, and don't stick your neck out unnecessarily. Do a general search and bring back all the data you can. That shouldn't arouse any suspicions."

"Do not worry," said Ducic with a creepy smile. "I will keep my neck as fully retracted as I am able. Thank you once again for physics discussions. I found them invigorating."

I gave him a wave as he retreated to his room, wishing I could say the same about our conversation, but I was more concerned about his statement of our friendship. Not that I was upset about it. Dorky though he was, I liked the guy. I just hoped I wouldn't have to betray his trust somewhere down the line.

21

I felt a light touch and a shake, originating at my left shoulder. When I opened my eyes, I found Carl standing over me. A message icon blinked in the corner of my vision.

"Hey, Rich," Carl said. "I didn't notice any random eye movement, so hopefully you weren't too deep into your sleep."

I suppressed a yawn, undid my cot straps, and moved into a sitting position. "No, I'm good. I was taking a power nap." I flicked open the message only to see an avalanche of documents pour out in list form. "Wowzers. Is this from Ducic?"

"You told me to wake you if anything came back," said Carl.

"Did you go through the files without me?"

"What do you think?" asked Carl.

We both did, said Paige. *I would've woken you myself, but you know I'm not plugged into that portion of your hypothalamus.*

"I'm not upset, if that's what you're thinking," I said. "I was hoping you would've already sifted through this stuff. Seriously, how many documents did Ducic send us? Three, four, five thousand?"

Try just shy of ten, said Paige. *Carl and I are still processing them all.*

"So," I asked. "What have you found?"

You want this one, Carl? said Paige. *I'll keep sifting.*

"Sure." Carl sat down in the swivel chair across from my bed, more out of convention than any need to rest his legs. "There's a lot of data covering all aspects of the attacks, the resulting manhunts—or ship hunts, rather, internal theories, security memos, damage control. The works. But you expressed an interest in the teams responsible for investigating the attacks, specifically the chain of command and what orders had been given to what parties, so let's start there. According to the records Ducic provided, the first two attacks were kept secret even within InterSTELLA, at least to individuals with the level of clearance available to Ducic—"

"Which is?" I asked.

"Level three," said Carl. "As if that means anything. Ducic's clearance was recently increased from a level one before he was assigned to us. The highest level is a five...I think. It's possible the knowledge of levels higher than that is known only to those with said levels of clearance."

"Right," I said. "Go on."

"As I was saying, the first attack shared within the InterSTELLA community was the third. From memos released after the fact, it sounds as if key security parties knew prior to that attack, but they didn't share it with top company officials until then. Perhaps they feared for their jobs or that they'd be mocked given the implausibility of the attacks. Either way, it was after the third raid that an emergency meeting was called among the board of directors. In it, InterSTELLA's chief operating officer, one Salvig Halloföl, explained the extent of the crisis and what was known at the time. After the conclusion of the meeting, he ordered the chief security officer, a man by the name of Kapono Nalani, to spearhead the investigations into the pirate attacks.

"Kapono Nalani in turn drew up an extensive plan of action which he sent to the head security officers at each of InterSTELLA's ships in the Sol and Tau Ceti systems, including the *Snowbell*. In it, he directed each security team to devote a full fifty percent of their man hours to the investigation, and he authorized funds to hire external teams to also take part in the investigation. For the record, Vijay Chatterjee is *not* the head of the *Snowbell's* security, but rather a senior officer. The true head, Ai Matsura, delegated the task of finding the *Snowbell's* external team to him."

"Wait. Back up a sec," I said. "External *teams*? We're not the only one?"

"Apparently not," said Carl. "There are several that have been recruited in the Sol system, and a memo from a ship by the name of the *Olsynium* shows a team is currently being put together on Cetif."

I scratched my head.

I know what you're thinking, said Paige.

"Of course you do," I said. "You're inside my head."

She ignored that. *You're trying to resolve your belief that our investigative team was put together with the intent that it would fail with the fact that many different such teams have been hired. And that Ducic, rather than being denied access to critical information, was granted* increased *access to files prior to being assigned to our team.*

"And I suppose you have a theory that would explain why?"

Look, Rich, said Paige. *I like your theories about the pirates and InterSTELLA subterfuge. They might even possess some kernel of truth. But I think it's more probable we're* not *being intentionally misled.*

"Then why has Vijay completely ignored us?" I said. "Why pair me, Tarja, and Ducic? Why not put together a team with a greater knowledge base, more experience, and a better chance of solving this thing?"

Convenience? offered Paige. *Think about it. What motive does Vijay have for putting a large amount of effort into assembling his team? He doesn't get a bonus if we solve the case, and as you might remember from Nalani's commands, all security forces must allot half their time to internal investigation of the pirate attacks. That doesn't mean Vijay's other work has magically disappeared. Don't you remember how curt and distracted he was? How stressed he seemed? I'll bet he chose you and Tarja based on availability rather than ability. Ducic probably got thrown in with us because Vijay has his own investigative team to run and didn't want to lose someone who might have relevant knowledge of warp travel. I'm sure he's ignored us thus far because he thinks we're a waste of time and resources.*

I glanced at Carl. "What do you think of all this?"

He shrugged. "It makes sense. Recall how persistent Vijay was that you take the job, and how relieved he was when you accepted it? That could be explained by your conspiracy theory in which he chose you for your ineptness—not that I'm saying you're inept by any means—but it could also be explained by the fact that you're the *only* private investigator on Cetie and he didn't want to waste any more time tracking down another man for the job."

I pursed my lips. Maybe Paige had a point. Maybe there wasn't a grand conspiracy brewing in the belly of InterSTELLA. Maybe we *had* been set up to fail—but not out of malice, rather out of convenience. It would explain a lot, but it would put us back at square one with the pirates, with the evidence leaning more toward them *actually* attacking the cargo freighters, by who knows what means, than them enacting an elaborate plot to infiltrate them from within.

I hate it when you think stuff like, 'Maybe Paige has a point,' said Paige. *When do I not* have *a point, and a good one at that?*

I shook my head. "You know I appreciate your insights, however snarky. Yours too, Carl, even without the snark. But right now I need time to think. Alone. Why don't you both give me a little space? Go over the rest of the files Ducic provided. Goodness knows that'll take long enough."

You want me to switch off? Paige sounded mortified.

"No, no," I said. "Just let me do some thinking on my own. It's good practice. Who knows—I might even have a revelation."

22

As it turned out, revelations were hard to come by.

I lay on my bunk, hoping answers would come to me. True to their words, Paige and Carl had stayed away, Carl in the physical sense and Paige in the mental. Unfortunately, their absence hadn't sparked a blaze in my neurons.

I stood and began to pace back and forth in the small quarters. Physical exertion often helped me think, and while I preferred a good weightlifting session or sparring match against a prospective kick boxer, a walk would have to do. At least the ship's acceleration had been constant for a while. Might as well take advantage of it while I could.

I clasped my hands behind my back as I walked. So. Pirates... How in the world had they pulled off the heists? As far as I could tell, I had to resolve three major elements. How had they gotten on board the ships in the first place, what had they done with the cargo, and where were they hiding now?

For the first point, either the pirates had matched the trajectories of their targets and boarded them mid-warp or they'd been onboard the entire time. Either possibility posed major problems. The former, while physically possible as told by Ducic, seemed practically *im*possible. The technology needed to effectively pull off such a feat didn't exist, and if it somehow did, there was no reason to believe it would be in the hands of a crew as foul-mouthed and inurbane as that captained by commander Horatio. However, the amount of coordination, subterfuge, and chicanery needed to successfully pull off inside jobs to rob *six* different InterSTELLA freighters, each with their own crews and chains of command, seemed equally as unlikely.

At first glance, the situation with the cargo seemed much easier. Either the pirates took it for their own gain, or they disposed of it through the warp bubble. The former made more immediate sense, but it was impossible without the technological leap theorized by Ducic, which to me meant the latter was the more logical choice. But why would they do that? I liked my theory about someone planning to scuttle InterSTELLA from within and massively shorting InterSTELLA stock, but Paige hadn't found any evidence of a company official taking up such a position in the stock markets. Besides, if said official were the mastermind behind the operation, how would they convince so many crewmen and women, themselves InterSTELLA employees, to engage in an act that would immeasurably harm the company?

Finally there was the issue of the pirates' physical location. Tarja was right. They had to be hiding *some-*

where. The asteroid belt was as good a guess as any, just as the Sol system's asteroid belt would be, but the pirates wouldn't be able to drop in and out of warp within the belt without the aforementioned technical advancements. From Vijay's own word and the documents obtained through Ducic, it appeared as if InterSTELLA scouts had been unable to find evidence of the pirates' travels either between or on either side of Sol and Tau Ceti. That indicated they must be somewhere *within* the systems. But where? And how could they possibly enter and exit warp without the InterSTELLA scouts noticing? Wouldn't they leave energy signatures? Maybe they wouldn't if they had their mystical advanced Alcubierre drive tech, but I doubted it.

My feet wore a groove into the floor, but still I paced. What if Ducic, Tarja, and I all made good points, but none of us had hit the nail on the head yet? What if the truth of the pirates' attacks lay somewhere in the middle? For example, what if the pirates possessed some level of advanced technology, but not to the level Ducic proposed. Maybe the pirates were good at hiding their tracks—eliminating their warp signatures somehow. Tarja had been right about the presence of thieves on that asteroid. If the pirates could mask their warp signatures, they could hide in the asteroid belt through more conventional means. I couldn't recall what the paths of the other freighters that had been targeted looked like, but given they'd all carried heavy metals, chances were they originated in fields of space debris. And certainly, I had to be right about the level of Inter-STELLA involvement. No way the attacks succeeded without someone relaying the pirates the information they needed about the freighters and their flight patterns.

Rich?

I paused in mid step. *Yes, Paige?*

Sorry to bother you, but we finally got back some information I think might interest you.

The query on Tarja?

If Paige were capable of giving me the finger guns, I'm sure she would've. *Bingo.*

Well then? I said. *Don't make me pry it out of you.*

I ran an exhaustive search on her through the Cetie servenets, and I bounced it to simultaneously run on the Cetif servenets as well. Full record check. I even paid for a couple of premium services that provide access to government files your private investigator's license alone doesn't. And...

I'll provide the drumroll. I tapped my fingers on the desk.

Nothing. Her record looks totally clean. Nothing that would conflict with the story she's told us.

Nothing? I said. *Please tell me there's a 'but.'*

Oh there's a 'but,' said Paige with a mental wink. *If we were running a simple background check, it wouldn't have taken as long as it has to get the information back. What took most of the time was running the lip-reading, statistical analysis, and cross-referencing programs I instructed the Cetie servenets to. Turns out the second pirate Tarja shot on TCA 133649 was, with a forty three percent likelihood, mouthing the word 'Banshee.' That alone didn't get us anywhere, but when we cross-referenced the term with the names of the pirates she mentioned in passing to you before—Tellerman Bundy, the Tryzekis, Paul 'The Cross' Richardson, and Korvik Durulaque—we got some hits. A bunch of them. Turns out 'Banshee'* is the name of a well-known smuggler who at one point—and this is hearsay—was robbed by the pirates Richardson, Durulaque, and if I'm not mistaken, the two guys you found on TCA 133649.

Get out of town, I said. Tarja's a smuggler?

Smuggler turned bounty hunter, said Paige. There's no question of her current occupation. She's brought in some highly wanted individuals.

I recalled Tarja's reluctance to discuss Richardson and Durulaque, and her obvious vendetta against the pirates on that floating hunk of space rock. So what did those guys steal from her?

No idea, said Paige. But according to a multitude of public and private police reports, the Banshee was responsible for smuggling just about anything under the sun that could turn a profit. Guns, drugs, genetic tech, state secrets. Even animals.

Animals? I said.

That's right. One report had her smuggling crates of endangered Peliosian boilerfish and selling them to collectors. Or restaurants, depending on which source you believe.

What the heck is a Peliosian boilerfish? I asked.

A fish, of course. Medium sized, with brilliant orange and yellow diagonal stripes. Thrives in warm, high-salinity water. Supposedly tastes delicious but doesn't do well under conditions of aquaculture, which is why they're endangered. I think there's one in the Cetie spaceport aquarium, actually. Give me a sec.

It took less than that. My vision faded and was replaced with the feed from my own trip through the spaceport. I stood on one of the moving carpets, staring up into the tanks.

See it? said Paige. *To the left of the school of cuttlefish, behind the shark dotted by lampreys.*

I spotted it, but I didn't care. Something had clicked in my mind.

I blinked. "I need to talk to Tarja."

23

I found her in the cockpit, eyes glued to the displays as a half-dozen charts and graphs and readouts adjusted in real time to the data brought back by the ship's sensors. Apparently, she'd meant what she'd said about the warp signatures and hadn't been jostling us about the ship, messing with our gastrointestinal systems for kicks.

"Tarja," I said. "How's it hanging?"

She gave me a sideways glance. "Fine, I suppose. You make any progress with those access logs and engine records?"

"To an extent," I said, "but that's not what I came to talk to you about."

Tarja rolled her eyes. "Not this again. Look, I'll admit you're not as vile and infuriating as I first made you out to be, but I'm here for the money. I don't have any desire to be friends, okay? If you're here to make small talk or pry into my childhood or share your passion for

God knows what, then you can head right back down that hatch."

"I don't need to ask about your past," I said, "but that's why I'm here. I was hoping you could answer a smuggling question."

Her look turned icy. "Pardon?"

"Paige and I ran a few search queries," I said. "You made it hard on us, but eventually we were able to uncover the truth, Tarja. Or should I say—Banshee."

She stood and took a step toward me, her shoulders tense. "No freaking way."

"Whoa," I said, reading her body language. "I'm not here to cause trouble. I don't care if you used to smuggle. Honestly, you could've been a pirate yourself in a past life and it wouldn't bother me, not so long as it stays in the past. That's your own business. I'm only bringing it up because I have a new theory about the pirate attacks and I thought someone with your *expertise* might be able to offer an informed opinion."

A puff of air escaped from Tarja's lips, and her shoulders relaxed. "That...wasn't what I expected to hear. It's actually a reasoned and compassionate response. Although I still don't know how in the world you connected me to my past life."

"I'm a private investigator," I said. "This is what I do. Or had you forgotten?"

"I hadn't forgotten," said Tarja as she sat back down. "I just hadn't thought you were particularly good at your job. I'm woman enough to admit I was wrong, though. So what's your new theory?"

"What if...the pirates were lampreys?"

"Come again?" said Tarja.

"Not literally, of course," I said. "But follow along with me. The tallest hurdle I've been trying to overcome is figuring out how the pirates got onboard the *Agapetes* and the other freighters in the first place. The idea that they matched their trajectories and somehow melded their warp bubble with their targets is pure science fiction as far as I'm concerned. But now that I've given it some thought, my idea that all six attacks were completed with the knowledge and assistance of the crews is almost as unbelievable. So what does that leave? Lampreys.

"What if the pirates managed to close in on the freighters undetected and latched onto them like lampreys? They'd have to do it before the freighters activated their Alcubierre drives, either at rest or under conditions of conventional thrust, but when the freighters enter warp, the bubble would form around the entire conjoined vessel, wouldn't it? From that point, the pirates would be free to attack the freighters at any point during the warp burn. Not that it would be easy, mind you. Maneuvering within the warp bubble would be difficult, but I think it could be done. What do you think?"

Tarja ran her tongue across her teeth and narrowed her eyes. "I mean...I think it's possible. I've heard of the technique before. Not from smugglers, to be honest, but from fighter pilots who'd hide on enemy dreadnaughts during battles that had turned sour. They'd wait for the action to die down and the enemy fighters to dock before blasting off at top speed. I've never heard of anyone attempting that sort of thing during warp, but I don't see why it wouldn't work.

"The key would be the approach, though. The pirates would have to come in slowly, ideally at a constant speed until almost the last minute to avoid detection. But in an asteroid belt? They could hide on a small rock and make the hop quickly, perhaps without anyone being the wiser. Avoiding the external cameras would be difficult, but on a large freighter, if they knew the right spot and with a small enough ship, it might be possible."

Tarja nodded as she talked herself into it. "Yeah. I could see it. It's a plausible theory, but it doesn't explain all your problems."

"Such as?" I asked.

"Well, the cargo for one," said Tarja. "A ship—or two, or three—small enough to pull off the kind of stunt you've described wouldn't be near large enough to store all the cargo from a freighter like the *Agapetes*."

"It wouldn't have to," I said. "That's the beauty of it. The pirates could pack as much loot into their ships as they could and pitch the rest, just as I theorized. Ducic already looked at the energy logs from the *Agapetes*, and he said the Alcubierre drive's power draw fluctuated wildly during the pirate attack. According to him, that could be due to the tossing of matter through the back of the warp bubble. You have to admit, if it's what the pirates did, it's a great way to throw pursuers off their scent. It threw me for a loop."

"Well, perhaps you should have Ducic look at those energy draw logs one more time," said Tarja, "because if the *Agapetes* was hauling one or more pirate ships around on its back, the overall energy usage for its warp drive should be higher than normal. Maybe not a ton higher, because that's mostly size, not mass, dependant, and if the pirates are smart they're manning ships that have a low profile, but still. It should be noticeable."

"And that's exactly what Ducic noted," I said. "A slightly higher than expected energy draw for the ship during its warp burn. Of course, he also noted the higher energy usage could've been due to an inefficiency or a fault in his calculations, but this would provide a genuine physical reason for it."

Tarja cupped her chin and went silent. She stared out the cockpit's display, her eyes focused on something far away or perhaps nothing at all. Eventually she turned back to me. "Alright. You've convinced me. But I don't see what good it does us. Let's say the pirates are here in the asteroid belt, or somewhere in Sol's equivalent. That still doesn't provide us any way to track them, not without them entering or exiting warp themselves. Resonant cavity thrusters don't leave traceable energy signatures like warp travel does."

I smiled. "True. I don't think we'll be able to track them down. But we might not have to."

Tarja lifted an eyebrow. "How so?"

"I had Paige check the documents Ducic obtained from InterSTELLA," I said. "As it turns out, the ship that was most recently attacked, the *Bulrush*, was in transit from Sol to Tau Ceti. If we're right, that means they're probably here, hiding in the asteroid belt. They may be looking for their next target, and what better target than the *Agapetes*?"

"You really think they'd risk hitting the same target twice?" said Tarja.

"Why not? Vijay said they've targeted ships carrying loads of heavy metals and ships that aren't well guarded. Well, the *Agapetes* is filling back up with exactly what the pirates are after. Tungsten."

"And it's been heavily reinforced," said Tarja. "I don't think they've increased the crew since the last attack, but you couldn't have missed that every member is packing heat. Those pistols weren't set to stun, either."

"But how would the pirates know that?"

The edge of Tarja's lip curled down in a frown. "I'm listening."

"I'm still convinced there's an inside man directing the pirates toward their targets," I said. "How else would they know which freighters carried the loads they desired and which ships weren't properly defended? But I no longer think the inside man—or woman—is onboard the ships in question. It has to be someone else. Someone with access to InterSTELLA's internal bookkeeping. Probably a desk jockey whose job it is to make sure ships don't crash into each other during their runs. This individual is probably looking for targets for the next attack. All we have to do it modify the logs to show the *Agapetes* suffered a loss of crew for some reason. That would make it look ripe for the picking."

"And how do you plan on doing that?" Tarja asked. "Do you plan on asking Captain Rhees really nicely to see if she'd modify the records to reflect that little lie? Or do you fancy yourself an all-galaxy hacker?"

I shook my head. "No way. Rhees hates me. But I doubt we'd have to hack anything. All we'd need is the appropriate clearance."

"And you think your chances of sweet talking Ducic are better than your chances with Rhees?"

"Well, yes," I said. "But I don't think Ducic is going to go for it either. He's too by the book."

"So?"

I smiled. "When Ducic sent the query to the *Snowbell* for all the internal InterSTELLA files relevant to the piracy, he had to submit his clearance along with his request. That query was routed though the *Samus Aran's* internal computer, was it not?"

Tarja snorted. "You're devious. But I'd imagine he encrypted his clearance pass code when he sent the query."

"Did he?" I asked.

Tarja's eyes glazed as she checked. It didn't take her long. "Ha. Nope. Unbelievable."

Bah, said Paige. *There goes my chance to show off my leet hacking skills.*

"Well there you go," I said. "Sounds like we have a plan."

"Maybe you do," said Tarja. "I'm still not entirely sure what you plan on doing with this information."

"Isn't it obvious?" I said. "We're going to ingratiate ourselves to Captain Rhees and get back onboard the *Agapetes* to try and catch the pirates in the act. Well, maybe not ingratiate ourselves to Rhees, per se. But I think if I give Vijay a convincing enough argument, he might be able to go over her head to ensure our passage on the freighter's upcoming trip to Sol."

"You're serious?" said Tarja. "You want to go up against the pirates alone?"

"Not alone," I said. "I'll have the whole crew of the *Agapetes* at my back. Not to mention you, and you're worth like ten of them, right?"

"Flattery will get you nowhere."

"Come on," I said. "You know you want to test your skills against these guys to see where you stack up. Besides, aren't you curious? We could be on the verge of unraveling a mystery that's eluded the collective minds of the galaxy's largest corporation."

"You're appealing to my sense of mystery?" Tarja laughed. "You don't know me very well."

"That was a joke. But I did figure you'd take part for the same reason you signed on in the first place." I rubbed the tips of my fingers against my thumb.

Tarja chuckled. "Maybe you understand me after all. Fine. I'll turn this ship around and head to Varuna. But it's up to you to take care of everything else."

24

Tarja stood just inside the airlock door of the *Samus Aran*, while Carl, Ducic, and I waited to gain entry to the *Agapetes*.

"Remember," said Tarja. "Be polite and gracious, and above all else, don't act like a giant jackass."

I glanced at Carl. "Am I the only one who sees the irony in that statement?"

Tarja snorted, and the airlock door closed centimeters from my face.

"I rest my case." I turned and faced the exterior door as the pumps whirred to life.

"You aren't the only one," said Carl. "But I can see where she's coming from."

"And where is that?" I said. "The corner of Insensitive Avenue and My Daddy Never Loved Me Lane?"

Ducic tilted his head. His eyes narrowed, but thankfully he didn't ask.

"Tarja's warming up to you," said Carl. "She's merely upset about having to leave her baby behind."

"You mean the *Samus?*"

Carl nodded.

Tarja was dropping us off at the *Agapetes* because of our lack of a spacesuit for Ducic, otherwise we all would've parked the ship and made the trip over together. It's possible she also wanted one last moment alone with her love without being subject to our judgment.

I sighed. "I just wish I wasn't always the one on the receiving end of her ire. Ducic hasn't been burned even once. Not that I wish it on you, big guy."

"Thank you," said the Tak. "I also would rather not be immolated."

The pumps finished their cycle, and the exterior door opened. Urrupain and his impeccably shorn hair stood in front of us, his hand resting lazily against the pulse pistol at his hip. He wore the same navy blue uniform I'd seen him in previously—or at least an identical one. Even the frown on his face was the same.

"Am I the only one experiencing *déjà vu?*" I said.

He nodded at my torso. "Not everything is the same, I see. Should I expect difficulties?"

I glanced at the pulse pistol in my own shoulder holster. "What, this? Come on. I'm not wearing it because of you. I figured if you're all armed, I should be, too. We already fought off a pair of pirates not even twenty standard galactic hours ago. I don't want to make the mistake of being caught unawares."

He frowned, but he didn't comment on it. We'd sent Captain Rhees a detailed missive with our plans. Perhaps she'd shared them with him.

Urrupain nodded. "Head to the command center. I will follow this time."

We did as he asked, and not just because he was armed. I *did* want to make a good impression on Captain Rhees, and I hoped my obedience would help.

I let Carl lead the way because I knew he wouldn't accidentally take any wrong turns. Down the hallway we went, eventually packing back into the lift, spilling out, and heading up the ramp to the command room. There we found Captain Rhees, sitting in one of the chairs by the displays. Uche had disappeared.

We gathered in the center of the room. Urrupain positioned himself behind us to our right. Rhees sat, impervious, gazing into the reports overlaid on the screens.

Urrupain spoke not a word. Neither did Rhees. The silence began to stretch, and I became unsure of the protocol expected of me. I cleared my throat.

Rhees didn't turn. "I'm waiting."

I opened my mouth to ask what for, but I paused before I could insert either of my feet into my gaping maw. The fact was, I had a good inkling of what she was waiting for—the same thing anyone in her position would be.

"Look," I said. "I'm sorry. I went against your wishes the last time I was aboard your ship, and when confronted with that fact, I tried to hide it. If nothing else, I responded in a flippant and arrogant manner. I shouldn't have behaved that way. This is your ship, and from now on, I intend to obey all your rules and regulations—if you'll have me and my team, of course."

Rhees rose, turned, and stepped forward to face me. She regarded me studiously for a moment before speaking. "You know, Mr. Weed, given our prior interactions, I'd suspected you'd continue your irreverent behavior, but I'm glad to have been proven wrong. Apology accepted. And believe me, I'm glad to be saying that. I didn't want to have to disobey a direct order from a superior."

"You received word from Officer Chatterjee then?" I asked.

Rhees shook her head. "Not Chatterjee. His superior, Commander Matsura. You must've made a convincing argument, because she gave me no leeway in her short missive."

"I tried."

Much to Tarja's dismay, I'd made my case to Chatterjee to be let aboard the *Agapetes* for her next warp burst through an unheralded manner—by telling the truth, or at least most of it. I'd shared my lamprey theory with the man and explained how the *Agapetes* would present an appetizing target to the pirates if indeed they hid within the asteroid belt. I only left out the little *modification* Paige had successfully made to InterSTELLA's centralized travel database. I'm not entirely sure if Vijay believed my theory or if he simply wanted to get me out of his hair for a few weeks, but he said tagging along with the *Agapetes*' crew wouldn't hurt anything, so he'd take care of it.

Captain Rhees clasped her hands behind her back. "I, of course, read the statement Officer Matsura relayed to me about your theory, the one about the pirates piggybacking on our hull. It seems plausible, however unlikely, but answer me this. Do you have any *actual* evidence suggesting we're a target going forward, or is that pure speculation?"

"It's speculation," I admitted. "But informed nonetheless. Not that I'm in any position to give you advice, but if I were, I'd suggest proceeding with caution and trying to be prepared for anything. That's how I'm approaching this trip, anyway."

Rhees eyed my shoulder holster. "I can see that. And while I agree you're not in a position to advise me, I do agree with your general sentiments. I'll be sure to meet with my crew and advise them to stay armed and alert at all times, and I'll convey your theories to engineering. We'll keep an eye on our external surveillance systems, as well as our energy draws once we enter warp. *However*—" Rhees narrowed her eyes and turned down the thermostat. "—don't for a minute think because I'm letting you back aboard my ship and putting some weight behind your suggestions that you can disobey my wishes, either explicit or implicit. If I say march, I expect you to march. Don't interfere with my crew, their duties, or their individual wishes. And if I find out you're snooping in any of their private quarters again, well...let me remind you the *Agapetes* does have a brig, and it's not particularly pleasant to spend extended periods of time in. Do I make myself clear?"

I nodded. Rhees eyed Carl and Ducic, and they followed suit.

"Very well," said Rhees. "I'll take you at your word, so welcome aboard. Now to specifics. I've consolidated my crew into three of the ship's quarters, leaving one for all of you to share, including your bounty hunter companion. It may be tight, given Curator Ducic's anatomy, but you'll have to make do. Urrupain will escort you there, and if you have any questions, you can direct them to him.

"As far as our trip to Sol, we're waiting on the last of the cargo, but it should arrive shortly. Estimated departure is in just over ten standard galactic hours. As I've already made clear to you, I *hate* being late. So don't do anything to make us tardy. Understand?"

I indicated that I did, as did my companions, and Rhees dismissed us. Urrupain ushered us down the hallway and back to the lift.

As we all piled in, the grim-faced man broke his silence. "I must admit, I'm surprised to find you as mates for the duration of this trip, but if Captain Rhees accepts you, so do I. I'll lead you to your quarters and allow you to settle in."

The lift sprang to life. "Actually, Carl can take care of that," I said. "I was hoping you might be able to show me where I could practice my marksmanship." I patted the pulse pistol.

Urrupain eyed me curiously. "Why would you need to do that?"

"Preparedness, my friend." And that fact that my encounter with the pirates on the small, hollowed-out asteroid weighed heavily on my mind. If I was right and pirates attacked the *Agapetes* again, I'd need to be sharper than I was before. *Much* sharper.

25

I stood at a window, staring into the inky black sea of the cosmos. I could make out a few hundred gleaming points of light within, though I knew there were a hundred million more I couldn't see even in my narrow field of vision. A cluster in the middle of the porthole had caught my eye, and Paige, being the helpful soul she was, had superimposed the names of the brightest stars over my vision. Betelgeuse and Bellatrix, Alnitak and Alnilam and Mintaka, Rigel, Saiph, and Na'ir al Saif, all interspersed with a handful of other stars of greatly diminished luminosity.

You know, said Paige, *together these stars create the constellation known in antiquity as Orion. Alnitak, Alnilam, and Mintaka create Orion's Belt. Mintaka in particular was useful to early Earth cultures as its nightly rise and fall closely aligned with true east and west, respectively.*

I blinked and continued to stare into the abyss.

Paige took that as an invitation. *Sorry. A constellation is a group of stars that ancient cultures—*

I know what a constellation is.

Well, forgive me for assuming you didn't, she said. *They are, after all, a purely terrestrial phenomena.*

That much was true. Given cultures on planets other than Earth had developed in the post-computational age, they'd never developed their own constellations. Instead, we were all stuck with the original ones from antiquity, no matter how goofy they looked from our various vantage points in the far reaches of the galaxy.

Actually, said Paige, *the Orion constellation looks much the same here as it does on Earth. Of all the stars in the grouping, Bellatrix is the closest, and even that one is well over two hundred light years away from both Sol and Tau Ceti.*

I blinked. *You're telling me ancient humans actually thought that group of stars resembled a bear? They had more active imaginations than I thought.*

You're thinking of Ursa Major, said Paige. *Orion is supposed to be a man. I mean, really? Why would a bear wear a belt?*

I thought it was a metaphor, I said. *Either way, I think I've made my case.*

I heard the gentle clap of feet and turned to find Carl approaching. "Hey, Rich. Waiting to watch the shift?"

"The what now?" I said.

"The shift into warp," said Carl. "I assumed that was why you were at the window."

I vaguely recalled Captain Rhees coming over the intercom ten minutes ago notifying us we'd be transitioning soon. Not that it would involve much from my point of view. The stars would stretch and disappear behind the warp bubble, and while we'd briefly lose the benefits of the ship's pseudogravity, it would come back as soon as the Alcubierre drive's energy draw normalized.

"No," I told Carl. "I wasn't waiting for anything in particular. Just hanging out, I guess."

Carl's brows furrowed. "Is everything okay?"

"Why wouldn't it be?" I said. "I've made warp jumps before. I'm not irrationally afraid of the technology."

"Then why the long face?" Carl stroked an invisible beard, giving life to his metaphor.

I could lie to him and claim nothing was on my mind, but he was my best friend. Besides, if I wasn't fully truthful Paige was liable to rat me out. "I guess I'm wondering if I made the right choice."

"You're going to have to be more specific," said Carl. "You've made so many poor ones over the years."

"Thanks for the vote of confidence," I said. "I'm talking about forcing myself—ourselves—aboard this vessel and hoping for the best. Think about it. We're facing two possible outcomes. The first is I was wrong, either in my general conclusion about how the pirates performed their raids or in my assumption they'd hit the *Agapetes* again so soon after their most recent assault."

That, for the moment, appeared to be the most likely outcome. Tarja had ingratiated herself with the ship's crew and looked through the external surveillance footage and the energy readings from the resonant cavity thrusters. Not only had she failed to notice any pirate ships approaching our vessel, either before or after exiting the asteroid belt, but she hadn't noticed any changes in thrust requirements, which should change if we'd acquired a space leech.

"And if you are wrong?" said Carl. "What's the worst that happens? We waste a couple weeks in transit and we're no closer to solving the case?"

"Yes," I said, "and while I'm sure Tarja will happily fly around at warp speed collecting her daily stipend, I hold myself to a higher standard. But that isn't what I'm most concerned about. I'm more concerned about being right."

It's called impostor syndrome, said Paige. Get over it.

Carl followed Paige's communication, but he at least took my unease seriously. "You're questioning the wisdom of inviting an attack by pirates."

"I know we've talked about this," I said. "There are reasons not to be worried. The crew is better armed than last time and prepared for an attack. The ship's computers have been scanned for malignant software that could've given the pirates an in. And we have more people on our side this time, namely you, me, and Tarja. Ducic may be useless in a fight, but I've seen you scramble to protect me, and I've watched Tarja in action. No offense to you, but she's the one who really impressed."

"No offense taken," said Carl. "So what are you worried about? I mean, I'm worried, but that's a near constant state of affairs for me. I get on edge when you eat a meal too high in salt and cholesterol."

I shook my head. "I wonder if we've underestimated the pirates. Placed too much emphasis on their apparent non-violent nature and refusal to use lethal weaponry. What if that turns out to be a bad call? Or what if they're more adaptable than we've given them credit for? I've watched the holovids of the attacks, and each one played out in a predictable manner, which essentially means we don't know how they'll react under pressure. And we keep wondering about the pirates' level of tech. What if they're holding something in reserve? Something dangerous?"

Captain Rhees' voice come on over the ship's speakers. "T-minus one minute until warp entry. Prepare for momentary grav loss."

"Regardless of the reasons for your hesitation, it's too late to turn back now," said Carl. "But I wouldn't worry excessively. The crew's prepared. You've been working on your marksmanship. Ducic found a panic room to seal himself in should the pirates break through. And, of course, I'll be here to protect you."

I smiled. "I know you will. I'm glad to have you at my side. Wouldn't be an adventure if we weren't doing it together, would it?"

Carl nodded and returned the smile.

I turned my gaze back to the window as Captain Rhees counted down from ten over the intercom. At five, the pseudogravity cut out and my feet floated off the floor, and at one I felt a strange *shift*. The light of the stars outside the window stretched into lines before compressing down into nothing and disappearing behind a sheet of blackness. It wasn't more than a few seconds before the gravity kicked back in and settled me back down on the floor.

I kept my eyes trained out the now dark window. "You know what the worst part about thinking I'm right is?"

"What's that?" said Carl.

"Envisioning the pirate vessel, packed to the gills with our enemies, perched against the exterior of our ship." I tapped the bulwark with a finger. "All that separates us is a couple of metal hulls. Now we're stuck together for a full week, for better or worse, win or lose."

Carl rubbed his chin. "Now that you mention it, we didn't consider what we'd do with the captured pirates if we won, or what any pirates who escape our capture might do in the same situation."

I snorted. "And on that uplifting note, I'm going to find Ducic. Hopefully he and the engineers can provide encouraging information about the Alcubierre drive's energy draw—or terrifying information, depending on how you look at it."

26

I stared at the back of Tarja's bunk, because of course she'd claimed the top one. It was as smooth, white, and boring as it had been two seconds ago.

I drummed my fingers on my chest. Then I tried to drum up some anger about the bunk situation, but I'd run out of that a couple days ago, if ever I'd had any. After a careful perusal of my options, I settled for sighing and feeling sorry for myself.

Well this is fun, said Paige.

I didn't invite you to be a part of this, I said. *You don't have to sit around while I sulk—and yes, I'm aware that's what I'm doing.*

Uh...I'm kind of stuck in your head, said Paige, *so I do have to sit around and be a part of whatever it is you wish to subject us to. But you don't have to be morose. There's plenty of interactive Brain experiences we could dive into. I don't have quite the selection I normally do given my current servenet status, but I've got a nice virtual tour through the Cetib lava tubes we could take part in. Seeing as you've been complaining about the food non-stop, I could fire up one of the gourmet Gloatsperiences™ I have on file. Or if you're feeling frisky, I always have a racy simulation or two on hand. How about that one where the temperature and humidity regulators break aboard the Martian swimsuit models' space yacht and things get steamy?*

You do realize I have to share this room with Tarja and Ducic, right? I said.

You're right, said Paige. *That could get awkward. Best not let either of them see that, unless you have unrealized feelings for either you've neglected to share.*

I ignored that last part. *What am I going to do, Paige?*

Hopefully lay off me for a moment or two, she said.

What? Why?

Because I pinged Carl and he should be here any minute, she said. *I'm tired of listening to your moping and he's more compassionate than I am.*

On cue, the door to my quarters opened and Carl walked in. He leaned over, poked his head into my bunk, and frowned. "Yeah, I got the distress call. What is it now?"

I sat up and swung my feet over the side. "I was wrong, you know. The other day? When I was complaining about what would be worse, being right or wrong about the pirates? Well, being wrong is worse. I feel so foolish."

It had been three days as measured by the ship's internal chronometers since we'd entered warp, and during that time absolutely *nothing* had happened. No pirate attacks. No bumps or thumps in the still of the night. Not even so much as a dirty look on the part of Tarja. She'd been too busy familiarizing herself with the surroundings, claiming she'd need every advantage she could get in the event we did get attacked. Even Ducic had been hard to find, though he'd provided me with the ship's warp drive energy readings. They'd shown similar results as we'd seen previously, namely slightly higher than expected energy draws but nothing out of the ordinary. I'd held out hope they meant I'd been right about the pirates' piggybacking efforts, but as the hours stretched into days, those hopes had faded.

Carl sighed. "I see why Paige called for reinforcements. There's no point in beating yourself up over this. If you're right, you're right, and if you're wrong, you're wrong. A great deal of this profession is trial and error. It's not as if you're alone. All of InterSTELLA has been after these pirates, and they still haven't found hide nor hair of them."

"Yes, but I'm not a vast, intergalactic organization," I said. "I'm independent and versatile and edgy. I can pivot faster and make decisions quicker than they can."

Carl rolled his eyes. "I'm sure. Look, I don't even understand why you're upset. You don't know for a fact your assumptions about the pirates were wrong. The attacks on the other ships occurred anywhere from a few hours to four days into their warp bursts."

I blinked. "They did?"

"Yes," said Carl. "Didn't you read the full reports?"

"I, uh...watched the holovids."

"Come on, Rich," said Carl. "Get it together. And I mean that in more ways than one. You can't sit around in your room and mope all day."

"I get that," I said, "but I'm not built like you. I can't assign those thoughts to random subroutines in my

Brain. I need to actively get my mind off it, and the problem with that is there's nothing to *do* on this blasted ship. Trust me, I've tried. Everyone's busy, and there are only so many practice shots I can fire off, especially when it means suiting up and heading into the cargo bay every time."

According to Urrupain, Jones, and everyone else I'd bothered to ask, the cargo bay was the only place I could practice my shooting. The bright side was that even though it was tightly packed, the area was huge. I could place the targets fifty or a hundred meters away, and it wasn't under pseudogravity so it provided me with more of a challenge. I'd also gotten really good at performing space suit quick changes, for whatever that was worth.

Carl frowned. "Sure, don't ask me to hang out. Not like I mind."

"Oh, you know I didn't mean it that way," I said. "I spend all day, every day with you. And besides—"

The ship groaned and a jostle threatened to knock me off my bunk. The lights above flickered three or four times before returning to full strength.

I looked up. "What was that?"

Carl didn't have to answer. The repetitive *woop woop* of a siren began to sound, and Captain Rhees' voice crackled to life through the speakers. "All hands on deck! Those thieving bastards are back, so let's give them a warm welcome." Then via Brain: *Everyone patch into the ship's servenets to share visual feeds. With any luck that'll give us one more advantage.*

I jumped up and rushed out of my quarters, Carl hot on my heels. Thoughts raced through my mind as I ran down the corridor almost faster than I could process them. The pirates were attacking? Holy crap. I'd been right! They'd perched on our hull all along waiting for the moment to strike. Now that moment had arrived. Was I ready? I glanced at my holder. Pistol? Check. Body armor? I didn't have any of that. But a faithful android companion and potential human shield? Check. Where was Tarja? I might need her help. What about Ducic? Was he holed up in the panic room? Hopefully the guy wouldn't suffer a heart attack—assuming he was able to with his physiology.

I turned a corner and found two of the *Agapetes'* crew, Kass and Wilkins, at the doors to a lift, pistols drawn. I caught them in mid conversation.

"—bizarre. It's as if we weren't even here," said Wilkins. "I can't get a response out of it at all."

Kass's eyes had a faraway quality to them. "Looks like the pirates are ready for decompression tactics this time. Most are in full suits. The rest have on respirators." She blinked and eyed Wilkins, who slammed the lift door with the butt of his gun. "Forget it. Take the hatch. We don't want to get caught in a small space anyway."

The pair finally noticed me.

"You. Weed." Wilkins gestured at me with his pulse pistol. "Take the portside maintenance hatch to the main level. We'll take the starboard side. Circle around by the cargo bay. Make sure the pirates entering through the hold don't flank us."

I nodded, trying to hide my underlying fear. "Got it."

"And use manual door overrides if you have to," called Kass as she set off down the hall. "Looks like security access is going wonky again. Seriously, how the *hell* did those pirates crack our system..."

Carl grabbed my arm. "Follow me. I know the ship's layout better than you. And stay behind me if things get hairy."

"Don't try to be a hero," I said. "Pulse rounds aren't good for you either."

"It takes a lot more charge to down me than it does you. And my parts are more easily replaceable than yours. Besides, I'm running active dissipation protocols and wearing electrically conductive shoes."

"Dang," I said. "You thought ahead."

Carl smiled.

We ran down the hall and found the portside hatch. Carl dropped down the ladder to the main level first and I followed. As my feet hit the floor, I pulled my pulse pistol and checked the setting. Stun. Good. I wasn't ready to use lethal force, and hopefully I wouldn't find myself in a situation where I'd have to.

I glanced down the corridor toward the cargo bay. Behind the steady *woop woop* of the siren, I could hear other things. Shouted commands and curses. The heavy thump of boot-clad feet on the *Agapetes'* floors. The crackle of pulse rounds discharging into the air as they made contact with hard surfaces. No whistles of projectiles flying past my head, though. Not yet, anyway.

Carl and I crept forward toward the hallway by the cargo bay, me with my pistol drawn and held at the ready. The sounds of fighting intensified, but still we didn't run into any opposition. Where was everyone?

Good question, said Paige. *I'd give you a sneak peek, but whatever the pirates are pulling is messing with the Agapetes' servenets. I'm only getting snippets from Rhees and Jones and the rest. Before you ask, I have no idea what happened to Tarja. Same deal with the ship's holorecorders. I'm sending what I can cull to Carl, but I'll save you from it. Might give you epilepsy.*

Just give me the highlights, then, I said.

Rhees and Urrupain are putting up a hell of a fight at the intersection outside the first airlock, but the pirates climbed in through a secondary lock, too. They're mostly outfitted in full suits, and they came in hot, pistols firing. All pulse rounds, by the looks of it. Fillion and Wong were fighting a losing battle there, but it looks like Wilkins and Kass just arrived to provide backup. No idea where Jones or Vijitpongpun are.

So what am I walking into? I asked.

Those sounds are from Kass's group. But you need to be on your toes. There's a path whereby the suited pirates could double back and come your way. I don't know if they're aware of it, but if Kass and company push them hard enough they might force them on top of you.

Dang it, I said. *I should've asked Kass to come with me.*

We crept along the corridor adjacent to the cargo bay past windows that showed a glimpse of the hold, densely packed with blocks of unrefined ore strapped into place by netting and tie down straps. The yells coalesced into recognizable words and commands. I pressed myself against the wall, half hidden behind Carl. I readied my pistol and prepared myself for a fight, but as we passed the final airlock through which Tarja and I had first entered the cargo bay under Uche's supervision, I stopped and gaped.

A swarm of bots was cleaning out the hold, one column at a time. They worked with absurd efficiency, cutting ties and straps and using their miniature thrusters to great effect in the hold's zero gravity. Their well-coordinated dance enthralled me, but as captivating as they were, they weren't what caught my eye.

The bots had cleared enough of the cargo bay for me to look all the way across it, through the exterior doors, and into the inky darkness of space and pitch black veil of the warp bubble beyond.

Except I *wasn't* staring into the inky darkness of space and pitch black veil of the warp bubble. I was staring into another cargo hold, at least as large as the *Agapetes'* own.

There was *definitely* another ship docked to us.

While I rested my jaw against my chest and tried to figure out what that meant for my theories, a trio of pirates in metallic green suits launched themselves from the lip of their cargo bay into our own. They glanced first at the conga line of cargo, then at the swarm of loader bots, and finally at me.

Thanks to my ocular implants, I could make them out even at a distance, although the glare off their helmets meant I couldn't see their faces or get a good grasp of their intentions.

I learned all I needed to know when they lifted their pulse carbines and fired.

I threw myself to the ground as a force of habit, but the pulse rounds plunked harmlessly off the Pseudaglas windows.

Plunked, and not crackled, I realized. Were the pirates using barbs rather than pure pulse shots?

I lifted my head and glanced at the window. It appeared unscathed, other than a single barb impaled in the center of the glass. It sputtered and sparked, then died.

"Are you alright?" asked Carl. He crouched next to me, under the window's lip.

"Yeah," I said. "I saw the pirates and their guns and instinct took over. We should keep moving. For all I know those three are going to head over to the nearby airlock and—"

I paused and stretched my ears. Between the woops of the siren, behind the curtain of curses and thumps and whistles coming from down the hall, lay something else. Something close. A faint whine.

I glanced at the barb in the window. The barest of cracks had sprouted from the center.

I gulped. "Oh, no."

27

A new siren sounded, an ear-splitting klaxon, and the doors at either end of the corridor slammed shut. I didn't have to ask Paige what it meant.

I dove toward the drawers near the airlock door and pulled open the one with my suit, on the left, third from the top. Thanks to my frequent marksmanship practice, it was still adjusted to my body proportions.

First foot in. Second foot. Over the back. Arms in the sleeves, gloves still attached. Zip seal the front. Helmet on. I don't think I'd ever moved so fast in my life.

It almost wasn't enough. As I clipped my oxygen bottle into place, I heard a bone-chilling crack. I lifted my head to find Carl, his hand pressed tight against the Pseudaglas on the other side of the implanted barb. The look on his face was one of relief, but it wasn't due to his efforts. The crack had propagated across the entire window face.

With a shattering crash, the window exploded outward. Air whooshed and screamed around me, scooping me up as if I were in a leaf in a tornado. The room swirled and I slammed my ribs into something—maybe the ceiling, maybe the lip of the window. Pain blossomed in my side, and I gritted my teeth. I spun and flew, and my stomach lurched as I left the pseudogravity field in the dust.

I saw a flash of metal, mesh, and straps and smashed into it back first, knocking the breath from my lungs. Somehow I grabbed hold of the netting before I bounced off. Loader bots scattered around me. With a grunt of exertion and a labored gasp, I turned and pulled myself into what I considered the right side up position.

I spotted a flash to my right: Carl, propelling himself at high speed from behind a girder to another bundle of cargo. A flurry of barbs trailed him, but none of them made contact.

You okay, Rich? asked Carl.

I took another breath. My side burned, but I needed the air. *Fine. Hurt a rib. I'll be okay.*

Carl's bundle of cargo was moving toward the shots—apparently the loader bots held space battles in low regard—so he launched himself to another.

I can see two of the attackers, said Carl. *You know I can't do anything other than protect you, so the offensive is up to you. I can scout, though. The first is to your right. Pop out and you should have a clean line of sight.*

My heart beat heavily in my chest while sweat beaded at my temples. My breath came short and my ribs hurt like hell. Taking on the pirates on the small

asteroid hadn't produced in me nearly as negative a reaction, but in that case I'd been caught off guard, forced
to react without time to think, and I'd had Tarja at my
fore. Here I was still trying to come to grips with not
dying in a painful decompression blast when suddenly I
found myself shot at by ruthless hijackers armed with
pulse carbines, and all I had was a—

Oh, crap. I said. *My pistol. I dropped it in my rush to get
the suit on.*

Carl launched himself to a new girder, again trailed
by barbed bolts crackling with electrical power. *Alright,
keep it together. I did a quick recap of my feed from the decompression event, and I didn't notice your pistol being sucked into
the cargo bay. It's possible it was caught against the suit
drawer you left open. Do you think you can propel yourself
back there to check?*

I looked. I wasn't far from the broken window—
much closer than Carl was, in any case. I popped my
head over the side of the cargo bundle to check on the
pirates' positions.

A handful of bolts whizzed over my head, and I
pulled back. *Dang it. The pirates know where I am. I can't risk
it.*

That's not good, said Carl. *If they've got a bead on you,
they'll close in on us soon. The only reason I imagine they haven't is because they think you're armed, too.*

Not good? Carl, old pal, you're not making me feel better.

For a moment, I endured his radio silence. Then:
Hang tight.

I did. With my back to the cargo bundle and my eyes
on the broken window, I wondered what Carl had up
his sleeve. I couldn't hear a thing, nor could I could I

pop my head out and take a look for fear of being shot and electrocuted—and not *just* disabled. Whatever rounds the pirates were firing flew at extreme velocity. If they'd cracked the ship's Pseudaglas, what would they do to my helmet's faceplate?

Carl flew past me with a speed I wasn't sure he was capable of, like an android missile. Bolts trailed after him like tracer rounds, thudding into the ship's hull around him—and into his surfboard, for lack of a better word.

He stood on a hunk of tungsten ore, big enough to hide his frame in profile. As he neared the window, he jumped off the block, pivoted off the ledge and disappeared behind the interior wall.

I gave him a whole two seconds to search. *Well?*

No dice, he said. *I can't find it. It must've been sucked out after all.*

More bolts peppered the wall, and my heart thumped even harder. *Can you get help?*

The corridor doors are locked down, said Carl. *There's no way to override them, and even if we could, that would vent another section of the ship. I could try to maneuver to one of the locks on the far side of the hold, but then I'd have to go around to reach the rest of the crew. I doubt there's time.*

I'm grasping at straws here, Carl. Give me something.

He peeked over the edge of the window lip and pulled back. The Brain missives couldn't convey the emotion in his voice, but I could sense the strain in his words. *The pirates are closing on your position. Rich...I...*

I tried to sound brave, but again, it was a Brain missive, so perhaps my fear wouldn't come through. *It's ok, pal. They're pulse rounds, right? Promise me you won't let me float off into the warp bubble.*

I must've struck whatever passed for a nerve in Carl's synthetic body. He launched himself out the broken window, grabbing the hunk of ore he'd used as a shield, and started flinging missiles in the direction of the pirates—spare oxygen tanks, by the looks of it. He cut a dashing figure, hair perfectly still in the vacuum and his face a mask of determination—until the pulse barb embedded itself in his forehead.

Carl jerked and spasmed and froze.

I gaped. *Carl? Carl?* Stuck as he was on that ore block and without air around him, he wouldn't have been able to dissipate much current, but one pulse barb? What kind of rounds were the pirates firing?

Carl and the ore shield floated past me on the far side. A shadow lengthened across my cargo bundle, that of an extended arm. I knew it was all over.

I forced myself to look as the pirate's metallic green form floated over the edge of my metal and mesh barrier. The glare didn't prevent me from seeing inside his helmet this time. He wore a brightly colored headpiece and had a sneer frozen across his face. He seemed to stare right through me, as if I weren't even there.

Of course, his sneer wasn't the only part of his face that was frozen. He floated past me, without making any attempt to shoot me or even grab hold of the netting.

I felt something brush against my back. I screamed and turned, only to find Tarja sidled up next to me in her purple suit and with one of the pirate's carbines looped on a strap over her shoulder.

Thankfully, no one can hear you scream in space, even if you sound like a little girl.

Where the hell have you been? I asked.

Tarja held onto the netting with one hand and chopped her pulse pistol across her throat with the other. She mouthed something at me through her helmet, but of course I couldn't hear her.

I furrowed my eyebrows. Tarja wagged her finger at me and tapped her helmet.

Did you catch that? I asked Paige.

I'm not an expert on lip-reading or body language, she responded, *but that looked like 'No Brain.'*

Tarja launched herself off and fired a flurry of bolts.

Why wouldn't she want us to use Brain communication? I asked.

Off the top of my head? said Paige. *Could be because the pirates have hacked into the Agapetes' servenet. That would explain my difficulties establishing comm lines with the crew. If that were the case, the pirates might be able to geolocate us based on our messages.*

Oh, crap, I said. *I'll stay quiet.*

I'm not broadcasting our own conversations, she said. *We'll be fine.*

What about Carl? I asked. *What happened to him?*

Not sure, said Paige. *He cut out as soon as he got hit.*

I hazarded a glance over the edge of my cargo wall and found Carl, pressed against the wall by his ore shield. He wasn't moving.

We've got to do something, I said as I pulled back. *We need to save him.*

I can't believe I'm saying this, said Paige, *but right now, you need to trust Tarja. She's your only hope. And Carl's.*

She was right. If Tarja didn't take out the rest of the attackers, I was as good as toast.

I sat on my hands. It was the longest two minutes of my life.

I startled again as Tarja pulled herself over the edge of my cargo bundle. She held up three fingers, chopped her hand in the air, and gave me a thumbs up.

I took that to mean she'd been successful, but apparently she didn't want to risk any communications yet. I wanted to ask what the plan of action was, but I didn't know how to do that with hand signals. I settled for rolling my hands and shrugging.

She pointed at the two of us and gestured at the pirate's cargo bay, which was rapidly filling under the loader bots' efforts.

She wanted us to go to the pirate's ship? Why? Never mind. It didn't matter. I shook my head and pointed at Carl.

I could see her sigh and roll her eyes through her helmet, but she nodded. She pointed at the two of us again, then at Carl, then at the pirate's hold.

I still wasn't sure why she wanted us to head there, but if it meant she'd help me save Carl, I was willing to give it a shot. I nodded. Tarja gripped the side of the netting, propelled herself in the direction of my fallen comrade, and I followed suit.

28

I hefted the chunk of ore off Carl and pulled him away from the wall, his body still and lifeless. The rational portion of my mind tried to convince the rest he was fine, that the current merely triggered the failsafe set in place by his dissipation protocols, but at the same time, I couldn't recall ever seeing him like this. Carl didn't sleep. He didn't rest. He didn't get distracted and zone off. Even during charging he remained alert and capable, if somewhat restricted in his mobility.

I glanced at the barb sticking out of his forehead. Perhaps if I...

Tarja grabbed my wrist in a vice grip before I'd made it halfway there. She made eye contact and shook her head, then followed it with a goofy face and a pretend spasm. I got the idea.

I collected Carl and pushed off toward the pirate's cargo bay, following Tarja's lead. Luckily, no more pirates descended on us out of the woodwork—or plastic and metalwork. The interior of the pirate's hold had been fashioned of a different set of materials than our own, with lots of polished aluminum and a molded plastic that gleamed with an iridescent shimmer. It reminded me of the skin of a fancy sport cruiser, but in the hold, it composed entire trusses and beams. Surely something else strengthened it from within?

Swarms of loader bots ignored us as we passed them by, pausing in their tasks only long enough for us to snake through. I'm sure our delay would be catalogued and analyzed at a future date as a means to improve efficiency beyond the bots' already impressive levels.

Despite the differences in construction, the bay appeared to be laid out similar to our own with a pair of airlocks on opposite ends of the far wall from the bay doors. We floated over to the one on the right, but the exterior door didn't acknowledge our presence.

Figures, I thought. *Paige, any chance you can finagle this thing open?*

I wish I could, she replied, *but I can't even get a negative response out of the ship's servenet. To be honest, I'm not sure they have one. It's like I'm shouting into a void.*

Wonderful. I eyed Tarja. She seemed to be experiencing similar problems on her end. Thankfully, despite the pirates being, well...*pirates,* whoever they'd purchased or stolen their ship from hadn't completely ignored standard occupational safety guidelines. Tarja crossed to a panel on the airlock's side, slid it open, and grabbed the controls within. She primed the emergency door release system by turning the knob counter-clockwise ninety degrees and pumping the lever three times.

The exterior door released, allowing us to push it open the remainder of the way with our hands and enter the airlock. From there, all we had to do was repeat the process using the manual interior controls, force cycle the atmosphere, and pry open the interior door.

The pseudogravity cut in right before the door opened on the ship's interior. I dragged Carl inside and retracted my face panel. Tarja did the same.

"Think it's safe to talk?" I said.

Tarja shrugged. "Who knows. If this ship is anything like our own, there are holorecorders all over the place. Even if there aren't, a security system surely logged us manually opening the airlock. We need to move."

"Not so fast," I said. "I need to get Carl back online. As strong as I am, I can't carry him around under pseudogravity. He'll turn me into a liability."

"Leave him, then. We don't have time for this."

"Tarja. I *need* him back. He's my friend."

Tarja glanced up and down the hallway, her carbine still gripped in her hands. "Fine, but you need to be quick about it. Given your long, codependent bromance with this android, I'm assuming you know more about what to do in this situation than I do. So what's the plan?"

"Remove the barb," I said. "If he doesn't perk up automatically, I'll perform a hard reset on him. Won't take more than fifteen to thirty seconds."

"And if that fails?"

"Let's hope it doesn't."

Tarja leaned over and looked closely at the barb. "Doesn't seem to be sparking, so you should be okay. You're wearing non-conductive gloves, right?"

I shrugged. "Beats me. When it comes to spacesuits, you're the expert."

"Well I know for a fact mine are." Tarja reached out, plucked the barb from Carl's forehead, and flicked it to the ground. Nothing happened, to her or to Carl. "You're up, slugger."

I snaked the tip of my pinky finger into Carl's right ear canal, feeling for the reset button. When I found it, I held it down. After ten seconds, I felt a faint click. Then I pushed it again.

Nothing happened. Tarja and I passed a few tense seconds in silence before Carl's eyes snapped open.

"Rich?" His eyes darted back and forth, taking in the surroundings. "What happened?"

Air burst out of my lungs in a relieved sigh. I hadn't realized I'd been holding my breath. "Good to see you, too, pal. You had me worried for a minute. Or three or five."

"About seven," said Tarja, "but who's counting? Now can we get moving?"

Carl eyed the bounty hunter. "I can only speculate at this point, but I'm guessing I own you some thanks, both on my behalf and Rich's."

"Why do you assume I didn't already thank her?" I asked.

He lifted a brow. "Did you?"

"Don't make me regret resetting you."

"Are you two done?" said Tarja. "We need to move. It's not safe here."

Carl glanced at our surroundings once more. "I take it we're aboard the pirate vessel. Why?"

"Good question," I said. "Rebooting your limp carcass took precedent, but the thought had crossed my mind. Tarja?"

"Leverage," she said.

"*Leverage?*"

"Yes, leverage. What are you, a mynah bird?"

"Let's keep level heads," said Carl. "Tarja, can you bring us up to speed? Rich's and my connections to the *Agapetes'* servenet have been spotty to say the least."

"That's because the pirates torpedoed it," said Tarja. "I'm not sure how, but they've mostly blocked Brain communication to the ship's computer. Locked us out. Restricted access to a number of the *Agapetes'* basic systems. I had to force a couple doors just to get into the hold."

"What does this have to do with leverage?" I asked.

"I don't know how much of the fight you were able to follow," said Tarja, "but when I left, things weren't looking too good. I don't know what happened to Kass and Wilkins' team, but Rhees and Urrupain got overwhelmed. Captain Horatio and his men captured them, and let me tell you, they were *not* happy about our counterattack. I haven't spoken to them, but I have a feeling they're not going to be as merciful as they have in the past."

"Which still doesn't tell me a thing about leverage," I said.

"Are you dense?" said Tarja. "They've hacked the *Agapetes.* They've captured some if not all of her crew. They may not be feeling generous enough to let us go. We need leverage."

"Their ship," said Carl, nodding. "I'd guess all, or almost all, of their crew is on the *Agapetes* right now. If we could somehow gain a measure of control..."

"Exactly." Tarja removed the stolen pirate carbine from around her neck and tossed it to me, simultaneously drawing her pulse pistol from its holster. "So maybe now you understand my urgency. We need to find the ship's control room. I'm hoping it's deserted, but if it's not, you won't be much use without your pulse pistol. I also have no idea where it might be, but unless this ship has a different design than anything I've set foot on before, I'm guessing we should delve toward the center. Now follow me."

I did, as did Carl. Thanks to the lack of active shooting and my partner's return, my nerves had settled, but as our feet pounded against the floors of the empty corridors, primarily constructed out of more of the shimmery, brightly colored plastic from the cargo bay, I found myself having a hard time concentrating on the task at hand.

"Um...guys? Can we talk about this ship for a moment?"

"You mean the garish color scheme?" asked Tarja.

"I was thinking more about that fact that it's here at all," I said. "Docked to the *Agapetes*. While we're still in warp, as far as I can tell."

"Right," said Tarja. "That."

Carl gave me a sympathetic glance. "Apparently, InterSTELLA's intelligence was right all along. Go figure."

"But...*how?*" I said. "I thought we'd agreed warp bubble merging and space time compression matching technology didn't exist."

"Clearly, we were wrong," said Carl. "But look on the bright side. Ducic is going to be giddy as a school girl once he recovers from his panic attack."

"Can it," said Tarja. "Just because we're staying off Brain channels doesn't mean any pirates left aboard won't be able to track us by your yapping."

I took her advice. Tarja, fueled by some internal ship-oriented spidey-sense, led us down corridors, past the open doors of crew quarters and galleys. Part of me wondered how big the ship was and if Tarja's method wasn't simply trial and error, but within a minute or two of searching we entered a hallway that widened at the far end into a cylindrical room. Bright lights filled it, and I spotted the backs of a couple captain's chairs.

We rushed forward. A door slid shut in front of our faces, bare meters from the edge of the room. We turned, only to see another door clamp shut twenty paces behind us.

"*Son of a...*" Tarja slammed the butt of her gun against the wall.

I glanced at the walls by the door in front of us. I didn't see an emergency release. Same with the door behind us. "Think somebody trapped us manually? Or did we trigger an automatic failsafe?"

"Does it matter?" asked Tarja. "Come on, we need to figure out how to get out."

"It matters because if this was deliberate, there might be more bad stuff headed our way," I said. "Anything from knockout gas to a horde of armed pirates."

"Shut up and help me with the door, will you?" Tarja removed a multitool from a suit pocket and jabbed the end into the door's seal.

"Wait," said Carl. "Hear that?"

"Hear what?" I asked.

"A thump." He pointed past the door, in the direction of what we assumed was the command room.

Tarja and I followed his finger, and lacking x-ray vision, we subsequently stretched our ears. I didn't hear anything at first, but then...something. Footsteps?

The door shuddered, and I heard a grinding rasp, that of metal on metal.

Tarja stepped back and readied her pistol. "Weapons!"

I aimed my carbine at the seal. The door shook again and produced another grating screech. How many pirates lurked on the other side? Five? A dozen? What kind of weaponry would they carry? Would it even be worth it to fight? Maybe Tarja and I should lay down our arms and beg for mercy. Maybe—

Another screeching grind, and the door opened a few centimeters. A voice carried through the crack. A familiar one.

"Don't shoot, guys."

29

"Uche?" I said. "Is that you?"

On cue, the man's fingers slid through the gap and grasped the door. "Sure is. Now give me a hand with this. Pull on three, okay?"

Carl and I grasped opposite sides. Uche counted up, and we pulled. With the door's screeching protest filling our ears, we forced the panels apart.

Uche stood on the other side, outfitted in one of the same silver and grey InterSTELLA spacesuits I wore, a pulse pistol holstered at his side. As glad as I was to see him, I found myself confused. Had he really abandoned the *Agapetes'* crew? Could he be the inside man I'd worried about? I'd previously come to the conclusion the pirates' source wasn't aboard the ship but rather inside InterSTELLA headquarters, but I could've been mistaken. Of course, if he wasn't on our side, why was he helping us?

Tarja put things more concisely than I could've. "What the hell are you doing here?"

"I could ask you the same question," said Jones.

"But you didn't," said Tarja.

The chocolate-skinned man frowned. "I got caught in engineering when the pirates initiated their attack. When I tried to get out, I found my ship's access was blocked. Doors wouldn't even open for me, so I had to force them manually. I couldn't get ahold of Captain Rhees either. When I finally made contact, it was right as she was going down. She told me to loop around and reinforce Kass's team, so that's what I attempted, but I got cut off from them thanks to the lockdown caused by your broken cargo bay window incident.

"That's when I took matters into my own hands. Figuring Kass, Wilkins, and the rest were on their own, I suited up, followed you over here, cycled the airlock once you'd moved on, and skirted around to the ship's far side."

"Okay," said Tarja. "But why?"

Uche lifted a brow. "One word—"

"Leverage?" I said. "I bet it's leverage."

"Yes, actually." He seemed disappointed I'd stolen his thunder. He waved us through the doors into the command room.

"We could've used your help in the cargo bay," said Tarja.

"And I would've given it," said Uche, "if I'd been able to arrive in time. I didn't make it through the airlock until you were halfway into this ship."

That would explain why I hadn't seen him. "Why didn't you show your face before we took off in search of this place? Some backup would've been appreciated."

"No offense, but I used you as bait. Seeing how this turned out, you should be glad I did." Uche gestured to the floor, where we found a pirate paralyzed and sprawled across the floor. "He was following you closely through the security channels. Didn't catch me, though. Guess the airlock alarm didn't reset after you snuck through it."

Tarja gave the man a reluctant nod. "Good work, but we need to keep our guard up. There's no guarantee this chump was the only one left on board, not to mention we have no idea when the rest of the pirates will be back. We'll need to work fast. Find something we can use against the attackers."

"I'm with you," said Uche. "But the question is how. I've tried to interface with the ship's computer via Brain and gotten nothing but silence in return."

"We could hardwire our way into the systems," said Tarja. "We're in the control room. There should be a manual access station somewhere."

I looked around the room. For as much as it resembled the *Agapetes'* command station, with floor to ceiling displays and numerous outward-facing built in chairs, I didn't see any backup controls. Perhaps the pirates' ship was fully Brain controlled? I thought that was against code.

"You're proficient in manual overrides?" asked Uche.

"Not especially," said Tarja. "But barring a more radical, last ditch effort, I don't have a better idea."

"I do," said Uche. "We've got a prisoner now. Let's secure him and make him do our dirty work."

Uche hooked his arms under the unconscious pirate's armpits, lifted him, and dumped him into one of the chairs.

Carl lifted a finger. "You're...not planning on torturing this fellow, are you?"

"You're implying I *have* a plan," said Uche. "Someone find me some zips or PolyPly cord."

I checked my suit's pockets but didn't find much of anything. As I performed the check, the room faded around me. The back half darkened, and the other half merged into the *Agapetes'* own central command.

Uh...Paige.

Don't look at me, she said. *I'm not doing anything. Hidden holoprojectors, maybe?*

The scene before me was familiar yet new. Captain Rhees and Urrupain sat in the center of the room, tied back to back with disheveled hair and scrapes on their faces. Wilkins and Kass were there too, bloodied and battered, as was Ducic, cowering and shaking and squeezing his eyes shut as tight as they'd go. Behind them stood a number of pirates, grim scowls stretching their faces, and in the front, floating half-between the *Agapetes'* command room and our own, was Captain Horatio, again wearing a crisp shirt and short-sleeved suit jacket along with his colorful headgear.

He blinked. "Ah. Well, this 'splains why Marcus wasn't respondin'."

Tarja stepped forward into the projection. "The gig is up, Horatio. It's time to deal."

"The *gig's* up? *S'time to deal?* What the skrag ye's talkin' 'bout?" he said. "Who're ye's?"

Uche stepped forward. "Uche Jones. First mate of the *Agapetes.*"

"Ya, I remember ye's," said Horatio. "I's referrin' to the blonde space twig. Ye's weren't on the ship's roster. Same's fer the droid or the squat dumpy skragger in back."

Squat and dumpy? That wasn't very kind. But I noted what he said about the roster. Apparently, our ruse had worked.

"The name's Tarja Olli, and I'm your worst nightmare."

"Oh, I doubts it," said Horatio. "In fact, ye's seem a little, *mmm...rawr.*" He scratched at her with pretend claws.

"Cut the crap," said Uche. "You have something we want—my captain and crew—and we have something you want—this fellow. Marcus. So let's make a trade. No one needs to get hurt."

"Marcus?" Horatio laughed. "He's a skraggin' twit. Take 'im."

"We have your ship, too," said Tarja.

"Ye's do?" Horatio leaned in and tilted his head. "Tha's news to me. Rüdiger, why don'a you take a team back to the *Wumpus* 'an see jes how taken she is."

One of the men in back nodded and motioned for a few of the others to follow him. As he did so, Tarja holstered her pistol and unzipped the front of her space suit.

"Gramercy! Hold on, Rüdiger," said Horatio. "Might wanna wait fer this. Decided to offer somethin' a little more *visually appealin'* in trade?"

"Something like that." Tarja pulled open the front flaps of her suit and reached down to her belt. When she drew her hand out, she held a metal sphere about the size of an apple. She pressed a latch and the front of it pulsed with a red light.

"Good lord, woman, what are you doing?" said Uche.

"Know what this is?" asked Tarja. "M60 twenty megajoule combination tactical concussion and EMP grenade. It won't destroy your ship, but it should leave a nice hole in its belly. The cleanup wouldn't be any fun, I imagine."

Horatio's face darkened, and he took another step forward. "Listen 'ere ye's skraggin' two-faced daughter of an asteroid-miner. I don'a know how ye's lot found me, but right now I don't skraggin' care. I's tried to be nice. Seven attacks now and I's yet to murder one of ye's skraggers, much as I's wanted to after ye's spaced a handful of my men. Seven! An' this is the thanks I get? What, ye's think I won't tempt fate? Skrag causality an' consequences! Ye's wanna skrag with me? Get ready to taste the muzzle's fire."

He drew his pistol and turned to the tied up crew.

"No!" cried Uche. "Nobody needs to get hurt, not any more than they already are. Tarja, put that thing away. Horatio. You can have your ship. Hell, you can have the cargo. I don't care. All we want is the *Agapetes* and her crew back."

Horatio turned back to us, his jaw clenched. He waved at Tarja with the gun. "Deactivate that thing. Put her on the ground an' step back. Then we talk."

"I don't think you understand how hostage situations work," said Tarja. "If either of us gives up our leverage, we lose. And it's not like we're face to face. As soon as this cuts out, I could blow your ship's guts or you could waste the crew. The difference is I can detonate my grenade remotely."

"Tarja, please..." Uche's voice had grown higher pitched.

Horatio scowled. "Ney. The horse-faced asteroid-miner's daughter's right. So here's how this is gonna work. I'ma wait another...seventeen minutes 'til my bots empty ye'ss ship's cargo hold. Then me an' my men are gonna head back to our ship through the airlocks. We'll be bringing ye'ss skraggin' Captain with us. Any funny stuff, we space 'er an' grab the next in line. Meanwhile, y'es'll head back to ye'ss ship through the hold. I sense ye's anywhere near us, Captain or skragger nummer two or three or whatever dies. An' trust me, I'll know." He pointed to the holorecorders in the command room's ceiling. "If ye's do as I say, I gets my cargo an' nobody dies. Otherwise, lots of people die. Skrag, maybe we's all do! But that's a risk I knew I was gettin' into. Can ye's say the same?"

Uche butted in before Tarja could say anything. "It's a deal."

The pirate captain tapped the pistol against his fore-head. "Seventeen minutes. Horatio out."

The hologram faded and we returned to our surroundings. I glanced at the others. They looked as tense as I felt.

With a flick of her thumb, Tarja deactivated her grenade and returned it to her utility belt. "For the record, I don't like this. Not one bit."

"What?" I said. "That you had to resort to violence? Or that you think Horatio is going to double cross us."

"Neither, although we need to be aware of the latter as a possibility," said Tarja. "More that if this plays out as planned, we lose Horatio and the cargo and you and I lose our bounty."

Uche jabbed a finger at Tarja. "Don't even think about it."

"Think about what?"

"Anything other than the plan," said Uche. "This isn't a game, and there's more than money on the line. The lives of my captain and crew—my friends, I might add—are at stake here. *Do not* screw this up."

Tarja eyed the man warily.

I knew that look. "I'm with Uche, Tarja. We can't risk it, and not just for the others, which is a pretty darn good reason. If Horatio goes ballistic, what happens to the *Agapetes*? What happens to *us*?"

She took a deep breath and let it out slowly. "Fine. We'll have to hope we can track them down later—although given how much evidence they left after their past attacks, I'm not feeling confident about our chances." She flicked her hand down to her utility belt, paused for a little longer than necessary, then resealed the front. "Let's head back to the airlock. We'll wait there."

The next quarter hour was possibly the longest of my life. Every minute felt like ten. I tried to pass the time watching the loader bots' efforts through a porthole in the pirates' cargo bay, but I found myself constantly looking over my shoulder to check for attackers sneaking up from behind. Paige had started a countdown timer and superimposed it in the lower right of my vision, which didn't do anything to soothe my nerves. The bots shifted the last few bundles of cargo over with two minutes and change left on the clock, and the interior airlock doors flicked open automatically. Hopefully, that meant Horatio was a man of his word.

We shuffled inside, waited while the pumps cycled and the pseudogravity cut out, then exited in single file, making our way down a narrow corridor created by the stacks of ore that had overtaken the hold. As we reached the lip of the *Agapetes* and launched ourselves inside, Paige gave me a mental poke.

Rich. The Agapetes' servenet is back online, and without any problems as far as I can tell. I've got full access to the ship's recorders and the rest of the crew's feed.

I floated toward the far airlock, the one that didn't lead to an evacuated corridor in lockdown. *How's Rhees?*

See for yourself.

Paige superimposed Rhees' Brain feed over a portion of my own vision. I saw her through first person perspective, being dragged down a hallway close to the ship's airlocks. Urrupain, Wilkins, and Kass followed her, pistols holstered, shoulders tense and faces drawn.

I heard Horatio's voice. "That's it. Nay closer, ye's skrags!"

The crew stopped. I heard the puff of a door opening followed by Rhees' own grunt as she was thrown to the floor. She looked back at the airlock, giving me a good view of Horatio and his men retreating into their ship, guns drawn and pointed at the crew.

Horatio's face burned beet red, his eyes wild. Spittle flew as he shouted. "Don'a think this is over, ye's skraggers! I'll track ye's down, ye's an' that whore of a Saladian goat-herder who threatened my ship. Any place, anytime. Ye's can't hide. An' *trust me,* ye's'll rue the day ye's crossed paths with Captain Horatio Halloföl! Ye's hear me? *Rue the day!"*

The door snapped shut, and Paige cut the feed. *Rue the day? Who talks like that?*

I blinked. I was more interested by something else he'd said.

We neared the airlock. Uche skirted it and drifted to its side, where he wrapped his arm around a piece of netting hanging from the wall. He cut in via Brain. *Get over here. Grab hold.*

What about the airlock? I said.

Do it. NOW, he said.

I followed his lead, as did Tarja. As I slipped my arm into the netting, I felt the ship groan, probably from the pirate vessel's airlock releasing our own.

I snorted. *Were you worried about us losing our footing? We're not even under pseudo—*

A bright flash of light blinded me, and I felt the *Agapetes* shudder and shake. A blast of hot air pushed me against the wall and spun my head toward the back of the bay, giving me a brief glimpse of a roiling fireball that was quickly swallowed behind a veil of purest black.

30

The cargo bay doors slammed shut, but a cloud of debris had already entered the hold. Carl threw himself over me to protect me from the smaller pieces of high speed shrapnel, but they were few in number and dispersed rapidly. I'm not sure if any hit Carl, although a few smacked into the walls around us.

Airlock. Now, said Uche.

Carl flung me inside before I could protest, and Tarja flew in with her usual grace. The doors shut behind us, and the pumps whirred.

I turned to Tarja. *You blew them up? What the hell is wrong with you?*

It wasn't me.

Oh come on, I said. *I saw you palm something back in the pirate's control room, before you resealed your suit.*

Yeah, she said. *A tracker, which I planted outside the Wumpus's airlock and which I didn't tell anyone about so it wouldn't be found. If we were going to lose the bastards, it was the least I could do, even if the tracker's function is limited by light speed communications.*

I turned to Uche. He'd instructed us to hold on seconds before the blast. He'd also claimed to have followed us aboard the *Wumpus,* but none of us had noticed him doing so. What had he really been doing there?

The pumps finished cycling, and I snapped open my faceplate. "Uche. What the hell just happened?"

He retracted his own faceplate. "It would appear the pirates' vessel exploded."

"You think?" I said.

The airlock doors puffed open, and Uche took off down the corridor at a jog. I followed, shouting after him. "Hey! I'm talking to you."

He ignored me, racing through the corridors to the sound of the ship's alarm—a new one, not the cyclical *woop woop* of before but a more subdued *blare, stop, blare* pattern. His legs reached farther than my own, and I struggled to keep up.

Where the heck is he going? I asked Paige.

There's your answer.

Captain Rhees sprinted down the corridor toward us, flanked by Kass. Several welts marred the captain's face, and her lower lip had swelled to twice its normal size, but the injuries didn't seem to slow her in the least.

"Jones. Status report," she said.

"Damage in the cargo bay," he said. "Debris from the explosion nicked up the interior, but nothing structural as far as I can tell. Airlock two is operational. Shrapnel didn't compromise any of the corridor windows other than the one destroyed during the attack. Not as bad as it could be, to be honest."

"Good," said Rhees, "because we need you on level two. We've had multiple breaches. Exterior corridors two c, two e, and two f have all gone into lockdown, and according to the ship's computers, we're suffering a loss of pressure somewhere up there. Kass, grab your suit and go with him."

The ensign nodded. "Yes, Captain. But what about engineering?"

"Wilkins can handle the stress on the fusion reactor. The energy draw caused by those warp bubble peaks is already evening out. Right now that pressure leak is priority number one."

"Yes, sir." Kass darted off down the corridor in the direction we'd come, and Uche followed her. Rhees turned to go.

"Hold on a second," I said. "We need to talk."

Rhees eyed my space suit. "It's good you're staying prepared, but I don't need your help right now. Unless you know how to use a portable gas metal arc welder in vacuum and zero gravity, in which case, come with me."

"You blew up the pirate ship!" I said. "Are you insane? There were two or three dozen men aboard that vessel. Now they're dead. Vaporized. Atomized. Whatever."

Rhees' eyes narrowed. "Those thieving marauders got what they deserved."

"How can you be so cavalier about this?" I said. "Their blood is on your hands."

"No," she said, gritting her teeth and pointing to her face. "*My* blood is quite literally on *their* hands. Or it was before they exploded."

I couldn't argue that point. I'd been shot at, but I hadn't been tied up, beaten, savaged, and held at gunpoint—twice. "But what about us? You put every man, woman, and Tak aboard this ship at risk with that stunt. We could've been killed. Based on what you told Uche and Kass, we could *still* die. And what about the pirate's tech? I don't know how they did it, but the InterSTELLA brass were right. Those guys had warp drive technology nobody has ever seen. And you destroyed it!"

Rhees took a deep breath. "Look here, Mr. Weed. Officially, I have no idea what happened to those pirates. For all I know, their *advanced tech* caused their engine to overheat and rupture. Or maybe Miss Olli went behind your back on another of her personal vendettas. But I assure you I put the safety of my crew above all else, including my loyalty to my employer. If I thought a course of action would put our lives at risk, I wouldn't go through with it.

"Now as far as InterSTELLA is concerned, trust me when I tell you they'd much rather have the piracy situation dealt with than have access to improved Alcubierre drive technology. But that goes along with the territory. You don't need to get any stronger when you're already the top dog."

"You can't honestly expect me to believe that," I said. "That the ship blew up on accident. Uche was there. He brought the explosives with him. I mean, I didn't see him do it, but he must've. Somehow..."

Come to think of it, how *had* he planted the explosives? The pirates had hacked into the *Agapetes,* and they'd monitored everyone on board. There was no way he could've smuggled enough explosives onto the *Wumpus* to create that level of explosion without anyone noticing. Of course, they'd apparently lost track of Tarja while they swarmed me and Carl in the cargo bay, but I assumed that had more to do with a lack of attention on the part of the trio of pirates attacking me than a lack of overall surveillance. Besides, they'd started tracking us again when we broke through their airlock.

Uche claimed he used the airlock after us, that he broke in without their notice. Perhaps he had, but the destruction of the pirate's vessel had to have been premeditated, and how would he have known we'd go there ourselves, giving him a path to follow? There was no way.

Then I remembered. When we'd first explored the cargo bay and checked the doors, I'd turned to inspect the rest of the area. Uche had stopped me. Claimed he was busy and needed us to hurry. But what if he didn't want us to look at the cargo too closely. The loader bots surely hadn't. They'd been too busy moving it into the *Wumpus* with extreme efficiency.

Rhees eyed me sideways. "You seem distracted, and I have matters to attend to. I'd suggest you wait in your quarters and keep your suit on. And, if you're the pious sort, you might want to ask your deity of choice for help."

She stormed off. I turned around, still trying to figure out if I was right. Carl stood behind me, though Tarja had disappeared.

As difficult a time as I was having dealing with the events of the last few minutes, Carl, due to his subroutines, looked to be taking it worse.

"I still can't believe she did it," I said. "Blew them up. I mean...I guess I can. The crew must've been prepared, and Rhees must've been under orders. But to endanger her whole crew like that? It doesn't make sense."

Carl shook his head, his face drawn. "She had to Rich. It was the only way they could be sure."

"Of what?"

"The bomb they planted. It had to be triggered before the pirates left. A remote activation wouldn't have been possible once the warp bubble closed."

"You're right, I suppose. But...this isn't how I envisioned things ending." I sighed. "Come on. We should find Ducic. And maybe start praying."

The panicked blare of the ship's siren dogged us as we jogged back to our quarters.

31

I stood in my room, staring out one of the *Samus Aran's* windows. Far off in the distance, I thought I made out the gleam of the *Snowbell's* hull. It was a welcome sight, but I wouldn't be completely happy until I set foot back on Cetie and felt the planet's firm gravitational embrace.

The past few days had been harrowing, to say the least, but the first few hours had been the worst. I don't think I'd ever banish from my mind the sounds of the *Agapetes'* various sirens. Every time one had silenced, a new one had sprung from the ashes of the last, eager to take on its predecessor's message of panic and impending doom. The intermittent blare of the pressure loss alarm. The high pitched wail of the oxygenator's flow blockage alarm. The low droning of the emergency power systems signifying the switching of life support systems to battery power.

Things got worse before they got better. Roughly half the ship had to be shut down, pumped, and vented, first to ensure the pressure leaks—there'd been more than one—were resolved, second to preserve oxygen and filler gas for the remainder of the ship. A substantial portion of the ship's reserves had been lost in the immediate aftermath of the explosion, which meant we all got real cozy on the return warp trip, which hadn't included a stop in the Sol system.

Due to the timing of the pirate attack, we still had on the order of sixty percent of the trip left to complete. Given our lack of cargo and the *Agapetes'* precarious condition, Captain Rhees ordered we cut out of warp and return to Tau Ceti. Of course, that had ended up being another gut-clenching source of excitement, as the ship's Alcubierre drive hadn't immediately kicked in on the return burn due to a sudden loss of power. Thanks to quick thinking on the parts of Wilkins and Kass and my own prayers to a dozen different deities, the crew diverted enough power from other systems to get the initial push powered. From there we had three and a half days of smooth flying and hoping the ship wouldn't disintegrate under our feet before we exited warp and found an InterSTELLA support vehicle orbiting the asteroid belt.

Tarja had held it together better than I had, but when we finally set foot back on the *Samus*, she broke out in the biggest grin I'd ever seen. She'd flashed teeth and everything.

Once en route to the *Snowbell*, I'd finally calmed enough to do a little more digging, although it helped to be out of warp and in a position where Paige could send search queries again. Even with Ducic's password, we hadn't found any record of a supply ship making contact with the *Agapetes* prior to our own first contact with them, but Paige did come across a press release from a few weeks prior naming InterSTELLA the new official carrier for a major explosives manufacturer. It didn't take much to connect the dots.

Whoever had delivered the bomb and instructed Rhees and Jones in its usage must've had a higher clearance level than Ducic, but thankfully, that same clearance must've exceeded that of the pirates' inside man—someone I was now certain existed. Their presence explained why the *Agapetes* had been targeted following our doctoring of InterSTELLA's travel database, and Horatio had all but admitted to having access to those files when he noted the lack of Tarja's presence from the ship's roster. Part of me wondered how the mole would react when they found out about the pirates' demise, but if they were smart, they wouldn't do a thing. Because of our subterfuge, it was possible no one knew about them besides Tarja, Ducic, and me. Not that *they'd* know that, of course.

Tarja cut in on my thoughts via Brain. *Hey, folks. Meet me in the main cabin. Vijay's requesting a live holofeed.*

I frowned. *Why? Aren't we meeting him on the Snowbell?*

Your guess is as good as mine, Rich, said Tarja. *He pinged me with a meeting request. Gather in the cabin, will you?*

I moved away from the window and motioned to Carl, who stood at the side of my quarters. He'd kept me company over the past few days, even if most of it occurred in silence.

I found Tarja already seated on the wraparound bench seats, so I slid in across from her and made room for Carl. Ducic didn't trail me by far. Ever since the pirate attack, he'd kept to himself as much as possible, and when we'd interacted, he'd kept his speech curt and succinct. I couldn't blame him. I'd found the ordeal traumatic enough, and I was a rough and tumble guy who'd willingly signed on to the mission. I couldn't imagine Ducic had ever expected to be embroiled in such an adventure as he pursued his post-graduate physics degree.

I gave him a nod. "How are you holding up?"

His ears lay flat against his skull. I hadn't seen them up since before the fight. "I am primarily vertical, but thank you for your concern."

The holoprojector above us spun to life, superimposing Vijay and the cramped interior of his office over the center of our cabin.

Vijay looked up. "Ah. There we go. Perfect. Although, Ducic...could you shift a little to the side?"

Because he faced us, the Tak's rump hovered squarely in front of Vijay's desk.

"Apologies. I meant no offense, or display of sexual interest." He moved to the side.

"No offense, taken," said Vijay. "Actually, if I'm being honest, I'm glad to see you alive and well, even if it is from a less than flattering angle. I had a chance to go over Captain's Rhees' reports and...well, as I said, I'm glad you're all alive and in one piece."

"As are we," said Tarja. "So what's with the holomeeting?"

"You're close enough that the lag is negligible," said Vijay. "I had free time and I figured I wouldn't waste it. Besides, there's no need for you to hang around the *Snowbell* after dropping Ducic off. The business we need to attend to can be conducted via encrypted channel as easily as it can in person."

"And that business is?" I asked.

"Straight and to the point," said Vijay. "A man after my own heart. Very well. I had three points I wanted to discuss prior to the culmination of your contracts. First, I wanted to thank you for your service to InterSTELLA. You've solved a problem that's plagued us for months now, a problem that..."

He paused. After a delay, he snorted and shook his head.

"Is there a problem?" asked Tarja.

"No," said Vijay. "Far from it. I meant what I said. I'm sincerely grateful for your service. But even now, after reading Rhees' sworn affidavit and going over the ship's logs, I'm still having a hard time believing it. When you approached me with the idea of riding along with the *Agapetes* and her crew, I didn't think there was a snowflake's chance in Venus anything would come of it. Yet...here you are. Victorious. You were right, despite the odds. I don't know if you're extremely lucky or extremely talented. Maybe both. Either way, thank you."

I couldn't tell Vijay luck hadn't played a major role in our success without revealing how we'd tampered with InterSTELLA's flight logs, so I kept my mouth shut. Besides, perhaps luck *had* played a role. There must've been other ships the pirates could've targeted, right?

"We appreciate the thanks," said Tarja, "but I think the compensation we're after is a little more tangible."

Vijay nodded. "Which brings me to points two and three. When next you check your bank accounts, you'll find the bounties we agreed upon in your contracts have been deposited. Try not to let your eyeballs pop out of their sockets. Ducic, while you and I aren't eligible for bounty payments under the terms of our Inter-STELLA employment contracts, the powers that be were generous enough to provide us with substantial bonuses for our efforts. I don't know about you, but it looks my family is finally going to be taking that lavish trip to the Sirius system we've always talked about.

"One other important point stipulated in your contracts, Mr. Weed and Ms. Olli, is the confidentiality clause. As you can imagine, it's in InterSTELLA's best interests to keep the events that transpired aboard the *Agapetes,* as well as everything related to the incidents of piracy, under the staunchest of wraps. They say money talks, but in this case we wish it wouldn't. We've arranged for your bounty payments to appear to be winnings from a high-stakes *pai gow* tournament you both attended in the sunny, luxurious Bella Lavica casino orbiting the hot rock pile that is Cetib. Should you choose to mention to anyone, in any capacity, that your time spent over these past days wasn't spent at the Bella Lavica, you'll find yourself prosecuted to the utmost extent of intergalactic law and taken for every fraction of a SEU you're worth, which is a whole heck of a lot more than it was a day ago." Vijay smiled. "But, you'll still have our thanks either way."

"I don't think you have to worry about us," I said. "From everything I've gathered, Tarja seems adept at keeping secrets, and after my last case with GenBorn and RAAI Corp., I'm used to the hush hush nature of private investigation."

"Excellent," said Vijay. "Now, unless there's anything else you'd like to discuss before signing off...?"

Once again the thought of the remaining inside man hiding within InterSTELLA crossed my mind, but I couldn't bring up his or her presence without admitting to our tampering of the ship's travel logs. Was it even worth mentioning? The pirates had been dealt with. We'd been paid. The interloper wouldn't dare stick out his or her neck.

Ultimately, I kept my mouth shut.

Tarja gave Vijay a nod. "Nothing on my end. I can't say it was good working with you because we rarely saw you, but thanks for the hire."

"Not a problem," said Vijay. "If I need the services of a bounty hunter again, I'll come calling, but forgive me for hoping I'll never need to work with you again. Ducic. I'll see you soon."

With that, his holofeed flicked out, and I was left to wonder if I'd made the right choice.

32

The airlock door to the spaceport puffed open, greeting me with smells of industrial cleaner and a medley of assorted pungent alien musks. Carl stepped into the hallway, but I paused and turned.

Tarja leaned against the airlock seal, her arms crossed over her chest.

"So...I guess this is goodbye," I said.

"It would appear that way, yes."

Despite the bizarre set of circumstances we'd endured together, I found myself at a loss for words. "Thanks for letting me ride onboard the *Samus*. I probably owe you a few SEUs to cover my share of the fuel and snacks."

Tarja chuckled. "I'm willing to overlook it. Not only were expenses covered, but I think the final payout more than covers it. As much as I hate to admit it, I wouldn't have...*won that pai gow tournament* without your guidance, if you know what I mean."

"Yeah, I do. So what do you plan on doing with your earnings?"

Tarja shrugged. "I'm not sure. I might take a few years off. Travel the stars, see some sights. Relax and drink margaritas beachside somewhere, though that might not be the best idea with my complexion."

I blinked. "Did you say *years*?"

"Yeah, why not?" said Tarja. "Why? How are you planning on blowing through your newfound riches?"

Come to think of it, I'd never read the InterSTELLA contract Vijay had sent me via Brain. Paige had approved it, so I'd affixed my digital print and moved on.

"How much did we earn from our domino victories again?"

"You didn't even read the terms?" Tarja snorted. "You Cetieans with your government stipend payments. We won ten to the seventh spacebucks."

"Ten million SEUs?" Vijay had been right. My eyes did try to leave my face.

"Don't spend it all in once place," said Tarja.

"I'll try not to." Dazed, I turned to go.

"Rich."

I paused and glanced back. "Yes?"

"Look, I think it's safe to say I'm not much of a people person," said Tarja. "I don't warm up easily, and I don't give out praise, like, *ever*. So when I tell you you're not a bad guy, you should take that, frame it, and stick it on your wall. Hear me?"

I smiled and nodded. "You bet. See you around?"

She smiled back. "Not if I can help it."

The airlock door puffed shut behind me. I shook my head, but the smile on my lips lingered.

With Carl at my side, I made my way back through the spaceport's corridors, past the food courts and through the moving walkways surrounded by fish tanks, muscling my way through the crowds of humans and Taks and Diraxi of all shapes and sizes. Eventually, I returned to the spaceport's base where the climber stations were.

"Manage to get us tickets?" I asked Paige.

The next available seats weren't for another forty-five minutes. Sorry.

I found a pair of free chairs in the waiting area and settled down next to Carl. Crowds of individuals milled in front of me, moving to and fro. They pressed thick against one another, their excretions wicking into the air, most of them paying me no more attention than a passing drone.

Despite their presence, I felt surprisingly alone. I had Carl and Paige at my side, of course, but they were part of my default state. Oddly enough, I think said state had started to grow to include Tarja and Ducic's presence, foibles and all. Some part of me missed them.

Thanks for taking me and Carl for granted, said Paige. *And please, don't start with the waterworks. You know I hate tears.*

I'm not that bent out of shape, I said. *Just adjusting back to normal.*

And normal meant I had time to think without being disturbed. I flicked open my Brain interface and brought a pair of images into my ocular display. On the right I positioned a still shot of Captain Horatio taken from Captain Rhees' live Brain feed. On the left I placed a headshot from InterSTELLA's public servenet, that of their COO, Salvig Halloföl. Through Paige, I'd run a search query on Salvig, but nothing in particular had popped out. He came from a long line of InterSTELLA employees, each more accomplished then the last, but nothing in the public domain hinted at anything underhanded in his past.

Can't leave those alone, can you? said Paige.

I still think I see a resemblance, I said. *Could be my imagination, but... I don't know.*

Well, it's rather fitting you brought those up, said Paige, *considering what I got back from the Cetie servenets.*

You have the results of the facial comparisons?

Just in, said Paige.

Well, what are you waiting for? I asked.

Okay, so I had the program run both Salvig and Horatio's facial features for similar traits. I was able to dig up older photos of Salvig for a more thorough analysis, but with Horatio we have just his current appearance. The results are as follows. Based on key genetic traits, the program estimates Horatio is related to Salvig with an overall probability of seven point four percent.

Seven percent? I said. *Dang. That seems low.*

It's not that simple, said Paige. *In this program, the overall probability of being related is generated by averaging through a weighted approach the individual probabilities by levels of separation. For example, it gives Horatio a three point three percent chance of being removed from Salvig by a single generation. The probabilities increase by separation up to a peak of twelve point nine percent at twelve generations removed before dropping again.*

So...what? I said. *Are you suggesting Horatio is Salvig's great-great-however many greats-grandson?*

Ten greats, said Paige. *And no, I'm not suggesting that. Even if that were somehow possible, the probability of its likelihood is still estimated at under thirteen percent.*

So what are *you suggesting?*

What do you mean? I'm relaying probabilities.

I sighed. *Paige, I know you too well. There's something on your mind you're not sharing. Or something on my mind. Whichever. You know what I mean.*

There was a pause. *Alright. Fine. But this is purely speculation, understand?*

Carl glanced at me. He hadn't interrupted, but he was being kept in the loop, and he was as curious as I was.

Sure, I said. *What is it?*

You know how we still don't understand how the pirates interfaced with the Agapetes at warp speed, or with any of the other InterSTELLA ships? said Paige. *It seems clear they did so though technological advancements, despite our theories to the contrary, so I went ahead and ran a few extra probabilistic scenarios without your knowledge. Not facial recognition stuff. General probabilistic analysis using metrics I generated based on the pirates' tactics, behavior, language, and other interpersonal parameters. Based on those inputs, I created a program to estimate their collective intelligence and estimate the chances of them crafting advanced Alcubierre technology on their own.*

And?

It's low, said Paige. *Really low. Like, miniscule. The chances are even lower that the pirates and only the pirates would have access to the technology if they didn't develop it, though the chances are higher that they've stolen the technology and others also have it but are hiding it. They're still really low* though. Fractions of a percent. Way lower than the chances of Salvig and Horatio being related.

Where are you going with this? I asked.

Remember the talk you had with Ducic? said Paige. Where you discussed Alcubierre drive technology and how someone might close on and match speed to a ship within a warp bubble?

You mean the conversation in which Ducic rambled about trajectories and vectors and the ship's chronometer before wandering off in a daze as he thought of something to investigate?

That's the one, said Paige. It struck me that even though Ducic mentioned to you the fluid nature of space time within the warp bubble, you never discussed something known as the chronology protection conjecture.

You know I have no idea what that is, I said.

One of the fundamental tenets of Alcubierre drive technology is that it creates closed time-like curves in space time, meaning, at least in theory, the technology could be used to enable backwards time travel. The chronology protection conjecture hypothesizes that in cases where the classical theory of general relativity allows them, quantum effects would intervene to eliminate this possibility. But it is, after all, a conjecture, meaning nobody can prove its validity except by disproving it.

Hold on, I said. You can't be suggesting what I think you're suggesting.

At this point I'd consider it the longest of long shots, said Paige, but consider the evidence. The attacks on InterSTELLA ships always occurred in pairs, usually in short succession. If backward time travel were possible, it makes sense it would occur in linear fashion. So the pirates travel back in time, attacking one ship along the path, then skip back forward in time, attacking another. *This would also explain why Inter-STELLA scouts never found warp exit signatures. Because there aren't any—not in this time period.*

Carl butted in. *Paige, I hold you in the utmost respect, but even I have to admit this is pretty fanciful.*

You think I don't know that? said Paige. *There's circumstantial evidence, too. The technology the pirates used to board InterSTELLA vessels mid-warp doesn't appear to be of this era. Neither do their clothes or their speech or mannerisms. And don't forget the fact that none of them appeared in any DNA or facial recognition databases. Or that they were using non-proprietary Brain technology and anti-aging antibodies.*

I'd forgotten about those last points. Okay. Just for kicks, let's assume you're onto something. But we need to think about more than possibilities. We need to consider motives. Even if it were possible, why would Horatio travel back in time to rob InterSTELLA ships?

I have no idea, said Paige. *But the interior of their vessel seemed to be composed mostly of organic materials and light metals. Maybe heavy metals are in high demand in the future. More telling is what the pirates didn't steal. They wouldn't have any use for our tech, clothes, or medical supplies. If anything, they'd want raw materials that hold their value. Or—and I'm getting creative here—what if the attacks were more personal. Salvig Halloföl follows a long line of successful Halloföls at InterSTELLA. Their family has been on an upward trajectory in that corporation for generations. Perhaps they've reached their peak, and future Halloföls won't view the company in as kind a light.*

I suppose that's plausible, said Carl, *but I think you're misrepresenting the results of the facial trait comparison. Genetic similarities extend backward through generations as eas-*

ily as they do forward. Assuming Horatio is related to Salvig, it's far more likely they both share a common ancestor than that Salvig is that common ancestor. And it would be far easier for me to believe that a distant relation of COO Halloföl is resentful of his cousin's success and wants a piece of it for himself. For all we know, Horatio approached Salvig, perhaps desiring a position of importance or to blackmail him, and was turned away. In his anger, he might've turned to piracy as a form of revenge.

I like your ingenuity, said Paige, *but that wouldn't explain the warp drive tech.*

I looked up at the clock over the climber station. We still had about twenty-five minutes until our scheduled departure.

You guys are making my head hurt, I said. *Can we drop it and bask in the fact that I made enough money to buy my own interstellar yacht?*

I would, said Paige, *but there's one final point I feel impelled to share.*

I sighed. *Fine. Lay it on me.*

Up until now, you've operated on the assumption the pirates targeted the ships they did because of some 'insider' InterSTELLA presence. It's a good assumption, but the pirates could've just as easily gotten the same information from historical records.

Yes, but—

I stopped myself in mid thought. It was true. The pirates had only targeted the *Agapetes* the second time after we changed the travel logs to make it a more appealing target. A potential future interloper might be able to access the data as easily as a modern one would. Plus, the entire pirate ordeal was being swept under the rug, known only to those with the highest levels of clearance. In all likelihood, there'd be no lasting records of which ships were attacked or that the pirates were killed during the second attack on the *Agapetes*.

Something gnawed at me. My decision not to share my suspicions about the inside man with Vijay. If I'd mentioned anything, InterSTELLA would've found out how Paige and I'd tampered with the travel logs, and they might've changed them back to accurately reflect the ship and her cargo. If they'd done so...*would the pirate attack I experienced have happened at all?*

I sat there in silence—the latter being a relative term given the cacophony erupting from the jumbled masses around me.

Eventually, Carl clapped me on the shoulder and gestured to the far side of the concourse. "There's a bar over there. We've still got time to grab a drink, if you'd like."

"Think that's a good idea given the upcoming climber ride?"

Carl shrugged. "You tell me. You seemed to acclimate pretty well to all the various gravity situations we encountered on the *Samus*."

"You're right," I said. "And if ever there was a time to tempt fate, I figure now is it."

Carl stood. I followed suit, chuckling at my own turn of phrase. *Tempt fate?* As if someone would drop out of the future to tell me whether or not having a drink was a good idea.

Then again, stranger things had happened. Or if Paige was right, *would happen.*

ABOUT THE AUTHOR

Alex P. Berg is a mystery, fantasy, and science fiction author, a scientist, and a heavy metal aficionado. Connect with him at www.alexpberg.com. If you'd like to be notified when new books are released, please sign up for his mailing list on his website. You will only be contacted when new books come out, your address will never be shared, and you can unsubscribe at any time.

Word of mouth is critical to author success. If you enjoyed this novel, please consider leaving a positive review on Amazon. Even if it's only a line or two, it would be a *huge* help. Thanks!

www.ingramcontent.com/pod-product-compliance
Lightning Source LLC
Chambersburg PA
CBHW021236250626
47155CB00008B/3044